D1648540

CALM
BEFORE
THE
STORM

BY
RYAN MULLANEY

ONE

SAMANTHA MILLNER WRIGGLED HER MUDDY toes against the cold concrete of the garage floor. A pitter-patter of rain fell steadily on the roof above, disturbed only by the occasional breeze. The chaos of the storm had diminished. Samantha listened, anticipating the howling winds to return, the sky to open and thunder to crash in the heavens above, but all she heard was the slight wheezing of her short breaths and the squish of mud between her toes.

Crouched against a derelict Chevy older than her by a generous number of years, Samantha kept her arm clutched to her side. A chill ran through her. She drew short, pained breaths. The ribs weren't broken, she told herself for the twentieth time. It just hurt like hell. She needed another minute. Just one more minute. Then she could stand up and figure out what to do.

Several minutes passed before she worked up the nerve to look at the damage she had sustained in the fall. Gingerly, she rolled up her soggy shirt. Fresh mud over sunshine-yellow. She strained through the dark to see, but the storm clouds had chased away the afternoon sun and left the garage in an early shadow. Daylight was fading fast.

She didn't know whether to feel better or worse about

that, but the pain wasn't as bad as before when she was holding back tears. Her breathing slowed as the adrenaline faded. For that, she felt better.

Samantha hugged her knees to her chest as closely as the pain would allow, her eyes cast down at the scummy floor. She didn't want to move, didn't want to believe what was happening was real. This morning, they were all having a good time eating breakfast at a mom-and-pop waffle house, hitting the road for an adventure she would recall fondly even decades later when her youth had long passed. How could they end up here? It was a day full of opportunity, of sand between her toes and the setting sun on the horizon, living it up with her friends and not having any care in the world.

She let her eyes close. The darkness soothed her thoughts. It was a friend in troubling times. She wanted nothing more than to sit there and wait it out, wait for somebody to come and fix everything, wait to wake up in the Jeep as they arrived at Rockaway Beach and realize she had been having a terrible nightmare.

But she knew better than to lie to herself. Nobody was coming to help. Nobody even knew where she was. She and her friends might as well be dead already.

Samantha squished her filthy fingers into the saturated pocket of her cut-offs. Her hand came out empty. No cell phone. *Shit.* It must still be in the Jeep.

A strange stroke of luck; had she had her phone with her, it would be drenched in mud and rain, likely inoperable. If it was still in the Jeep, safe and dry, it was her best hope of calling for help and getting her friends and herself to safety.

Samantha checked her pockets again. No keys, either.

Ted had the keys, and Ted was in the house. If the doors to the vehicle were locked, they were all screwed.

Ted was habitual. A perfectionist, always making certain everyone and everything was safe and secure. Tom him, there was a right way to do everything. Even in a moment of panic, he would almost positively lock up his possessions.

It was the first time Samantha hated how predictable he could be. She had no idea how to break into a locked car. Smashing the windows would make far too much noise, and the man with the shotgun would be outside in a heartbeat. Or worse, he would stay inside the house, and she would hear the sound of the 12-gauge from behind closed doors.

Her skin prickled at the thought.

At that moment, however, the only sound was the white-noise hiss of rain hitting the roof over her head. The wind had died down soon after the funnel cloud had nearly run their Jeep off the road. If Samantha wanted to get to the Jeep, now was her best shot. And she had to get to the Jeep. There was nobody else coming. Nobody else was going to call. It had to be her.

She raised a hand to grab the side mirror of the Chevy and pulled herself up with a grueling effort. A sharp pain shot through her side, and Samantha doubled over and dropped to her knees.

After a moment, she stood again, breathing the deepest breath she could take without passing out. Limp waves of mud-soaked hair dangled in front of her face, dripping.

Twenty-two years old, five foot three, a hundred and twenty-five pounds soaking wet, as she was, with wet earth slicked on her entire left side head to toe; Samantha stood no chance on her own against a grown man in a fair fight. She had never been in a physical fight in her entire life. Never threw or took a punch. The notion was so absurd it made Samantha laugh, the pain in her side driving daggers further in as she did. She forced herself to stop and catch her breath again.

She had only caught a fleeting glimpse of the man with the shotgun when he opened the door to the house and stepped out onto the wrap-around porch. He was of average height, perhaps slightly taller, with a sturdy build that suggested a life of early mornings and late nights of manual labor in the surrounding farmland. A strong frame, large hands, a heavy posture. No chance she could fight the shotgun away from this stranger.

Samantha had ducked behind the Jeep's tire to remain out of sight, and thankfully so. He had not seen her. Perhaps he was a much larger man, or perhaps smaller. She couldn't say for sure. Her memory was not to be trusted in her current state; she was tired, in pain, wet, cold, filthy, and, worst of all, alone.

One thing was certain: Samantha had to remain hidden. If the man with the shotgun knew she was hiding in the garage after seeing what she saw, her friends would be as good as dead. The less he knew about her, the better.

Juila wasn't healthy enough to put up a fight, but Bobby was most likely strong enough to handle the man if things got out of control and Ted was smart. He knew what to do to keep all of them safe. At least for now.

A strong gust of wind pounded the garage. The storm wasn't over yet. Samantha could feel her heart beating harder, faster. If the weather was getting worse, there was little time to act.

She spun around; eyes searching for something—anything—that could help her. Outside, darkness crept over the farm. Dim light spilling in through one small window of the garage's door grew inefficient. But it was a garage, god dammit, there had to be something she could use as a weapon if she fell into a life-or-death situation—something she was determined not to let happen, for her own sake, and that of her friends.

A tool cabinet in the far corner proved useless. Just small wrenches and worthless crap, unwieldy tools she could not identify. Some firewood stacked against the wall wouldn't do any good. On a workbench, she found a standard screwdriver with a six-inch shaft.

This will have to do. Samantha held the screwdriver in a white-knuckle grip—an improvised weapon if need be—and turned her focus to the door.

She took one step. Then another. One step at a time. It was all she could manage. Closer and closer she moved, until she could hear the rain blowing against the splintered door, hear the rattling of the ancient rusted hinges, the howl of storm-tossed winds that awaited her on the other side.

A cold breeze crept in from below the door and danced across Samantha's bare feet. A shiver crawled up her spine, all the way to the nape of her neck. The walls of the garage shuddered as a boom of thunder sounded above.

The storm, Samantha realized, was only just beginning.

TWO

TED STOOD IN THE CENTER of the living room with Bobby and Julia at his side. The man with the shotgun closed the front door and turned the deadbolt with a metallic *clack*, his eyes never leaving the trio of captives.

Julia stole a glance toward the kitchen. The body on the floor was not breathing. A splatter of what appeared to be fresh blood decorated the edge of the granite countertop and streaked down to where the dead man's skull rested in a crimson puddle.

It was Julia who reached the porch first, after abandoning the Jeep on the side of the road leading up to the home. Her tall, athletic frame peered through a front window to see if anyone was inside to let them in out of the storm. The interior was too dark to see anything but a pair of legs on the kitchen floor beyond the living room. She had turned to yell to Bobby that something was wrong, but the front door was already open and two barrels of a shotgun stared back at her.

They stood in the living room for what felt like several minutes before Ted cleared his throat to break the silence. "We didn't mean to intrude. We're just looking for a place to wait out the storm."

The man with the shotgun did not move. Ted wasn't even sure the man had heard him. The man stood by the door with the shotgun held on the three friends and an elsewhere look in his eyes.

"We can leave if you want," Bobby said, chancing a step forward.

The man snapped alert, shouldering the weapon in a heartbeat, freezing Bobby in his tracks. "No. You can stay. You have to stay. It's not safe out there," the man said. He spoke with unsettling restraint, as one unsure of what to do next.

Sweat matted the man's hair to his head. He stood tall, his shoulders broad. His hands twitched nervously, his feet not remaining still for long.

Ted noticed the body sprawled on the kitchen floor. His heart sank into his stomach, struck with a dread that they were not going to leave for quite some time.

But his mind wasn't on himself; his thoughts were with Samantha, stranded outside in the elements. Ted had no idea where she was, or the severity of her injury.

He'd heard the thud of a body hitting the wet ground. He turned as Samantha cried out, saw her on her knees clutching her side in agony. In a hurried exit from the Jeep, she had slipped, fallen, and landed on one of the large stones lining the path up to the house.

Ted hoped and prayed that her ribs were not broken, that no vital organs were damaged. If Samantha needed to get to a hospital, she was out of luck. She would have to be strong and deal with it for now, but Ted knew she wasn't strong. Not like her sister. Alice was the strong one, but Alice wasn't here, and wouldn't be coming.

The man snatched a handful of thick, black cable ties

from the coffee table and tossed them in the general area of the captives. They landed at Julia's feet.

The man pointed to the coffee table with the shotgun. "Put your cell phones on that table."

Ted, Bobby, and Julia all looked at one another. Neither of them braved an effort to do as commanded.

"I don't like to repeat myself," the man said in a tone that lacked patience. His hands twitched even more.

Julia turned a smoldering look to Bobby, who promptly rested a hand on her shoulder. "It's okay, baby. Let's just do this." He reached in his pocket, withdrew his phone and set it on the coffee table. His look shifted to Ted, who followed suit.

Once Ted's phone was on the table, Julia cursed under her breath and threw hers in with the others. She was not the type to let people tell her what to do. With death the only alternative, she had no choice but to do as instructed, as much as she hated it.

"And the keys to that Jeep, too. Which one of you has them?" The man panned his aim from Ted to Bobby to Julia.

"I do," said Ted. He slipped his hand in the pocket of his jeans—slowly—so as to not cause any alarm. He pulled out the keys and set them on the table next to the phones.

The man held his aim on Julia. "Pick up those ties and walk over to that radiator behind you."

Bobby glanced behind, filled with uncertainty.

The man again raised his voice. "The sooner we get this over with, the better it will be for everyone."

The words clicked with Ted. If they did as he said and didn't put up a fight, he might let them go. He had the chance to kill them right at that moment if he wanted to, but he didn't, and he didn't seem at all keen on dealing with any struggles.

The dead man in the kitchen was disconcerting, but it could have been an unfortunate accident. Was it another traveler in search of safety from the tornado? A friend? Relative? Intruder?

Ted didn't want to ask in fear of reigniting whatever rage had sparked the incident in the first place. That rage was likely still simmering inside the man who held their lives at the end of his shotgun. It was a risk Ted was not willing to take.

He walked back toward the radiator with Bobby, not wanting to comply with their captor but having no alternative recourse, and that was when they saw her.

In the dining room, set off from the living room and opposite the kitchen, there was a woman, hands tied behind her back to the doors of a mammoth, glass-fronted china cabinet. A single trail of blood was drawn from her forehead down to her cheek. She was gagged, unable to speak. Her eyes fluttered on the edge of consciousness. There she stood; an example of why struggling against this man was a bad idea.

Ted realized how wrong he was. This was no accident.

The man stepped toward Julia. "Your friends are going to sit down beside that radiator and you are going to tie them to it."

Julia gave him a hard look. She knew she'd regret anything that came out of her mouth, so she kept it shut and simply nodded. She took the cable ties as Ted sat down next to the radiator with his arms behind his back.

The radiator was old, heavy, painted over many times, chipped and cracked in more places than not. Everything in the house seemed like an antique. The floor was original hardwood that groaned under the weight of their footsteps. The walls shook with every wind gust that struck the outside. Even the furniture looked to be hand-me-downs from a previous generation.

Bobby sat with his back and arms to the radiator. Julia knelt beside him.

"It's okay, babe. Just do it. It's okay," Bobby said to reassure her as much as himself.

"Make it tight," said the man, supervising with the shotgun trained on Julia.

When she was finished tying Bobby, Julia tied Ted's wrists to the radiator. Tight, just like the man instructed. He saw everything she was doing. No way could she half-ass it and have a shoddy job slip by unnoticed. Ted wouldn't want to take that chance, anyway, whether the man was watching or not.

The man pointed Julia toward the railing of the stairs at the far corner of the room. "Over there," was all he said.

Ted and Bobby could do nothing but watch as Julia walked over to the stairs and slipped her hands behind her back and in-between the bars of the railing.

"Stay right there," the man ordered and set the shotgun down on the couch.

Bobby eyed the weapon with focused intensity. He tugged at his restraints, covertly so as not to draw attention to himself. Ted shot him a look that said, "No."

Bobby shook his head. He was having none of it. He didn't care what happened to himself, but seeing anything happen to Julia was out of the question. He would take whatever shot he could to keep her safe.

Ted's plan of not putting up a fight was already falling

to pieces.

The man took another cable tie from the floor and walked over to Julia. He stood uncomfortably close as he tied her wrists together.

"She can't stand up like that. She has a bad back. She has to sit down," Bobby called across the room.

The man seemed not to hear. His focus remained on Julia's hand, on the engagement ring on her finger.

He smiled, then put a hand on her shoulder and gently guided her to the floor in a seated position. The railing did not prevent her from sliding up to stand or down to sit, but she was secure.

The wind outside picked up. Rainfall poured with no indication of stopping. The man clicked on the TV and lowered the volume. Muted coverage of tornado damage gave some light to the darkening room.

Ted held his breath when the man picked up the shotgun again. Nobody said a word. The woman in the next room was still not fully awake, and doubtless unaware of what was going on around her.

The man with the shotgun stood in the center of the room, eyes dancing from one captive to the next. Wheels turned in his head as he silently formulated a plan for how to proceed from there.

The man's gaze fell to the Jeep keys on the coffee table. He took them and made for the front door, opened it halfway, then paused and turned back to address the room.

"If anyone is missing when I get back, the rest of you are going to suffer for it," he announced, and then he was gone.

THREE

WIND-TOSSED TWISTS OF strawberry-blonde locks were plastered to Samantha's face with mud and rain as she crouch-walked as fast as she could in the direction of the Jeep.

It was getting too dark for this early in the day, looked more like nightfall than an afternoon thunderstorm. The air was heavy with dirt and blown leaves and dust from the wheat fields that flanked the road leading to the old farmhouse.

Samantha was thankful for the dusky sky as she dashed for the vehicle. She would be harder to notice than if she was wandering around by daylight, but had it been daylight, she would still be in that Jeep, on the road, closer to her vacation destination than she was now.

Lightning blinked across the sky. A deep bass rumble of thunder followed close behind, refusing to fade. The sound trapped itself in Samantha's head, haunting her, threatening to go on forever.

She dropped to her knees upon reaching the side of the Jeep. It hurt to breathe. It hurt to move. It hurt when she did nothing. She shivered from the dampness of the clothes that clung tight to her skin, cold from the assault of the wind and the lack of anything more substantial than a tank-top and cut-off jean shorts. It hurt to shiver. She had lost her flip-flops somewhere in her scramble into the garage earlier and had not seen them since.

Her ribs throbbed from the effort of hurrying from the garage. The pain was unbearable. She hugged her bare arms, resting her head against the side of the vehicle, and closed her eyes.

Samantha wanted to sleep. She could, right there, if she wanted to, with no problem at all. Her body felt numb from head to toe, all but the ribs she was certain had cracked against a rock when she tumbled and fell.

She cursed herself. *Stupid, stupid, stupid. Why did you have to be so afraid? You're always afraid, afraid of everything.*

The cross-country trip had been Ted's idea. Samantha did not want to come, but she always found Ted persuasive. He was a great talker, excellent with words. Confident.

Childhood friends since before she could remember, Samantha did not consider Ted to be her best friend; she considered him to be her only true friend. Growing up as next-door neighbors had them spending much of their time together in the summer months when school was out. Samantha's older sister, Alice, was often with them, as her infatuation with Ted was no secret.

Ever the polar opposite of her elder sibling, Samantha kept her feelings private. She didn't believe she was blessed with the same attractive qualities as Alice. Alice was tall, always mature for her age; Samantha's height was below average. She often wished for a growth spurt, thinking it was coming in the next year, but it never did. She had lived her entire life under the belief that she wasn't good enough. Not for herself, and certainly not for Ted. She had such a huge role model in her sister, who showed Samantha the kind of person she hoped to one day become.

She wiped her eyes. Rain mingling with tears. She wanted to stay there, huddled in the warmth of her memories, the comfort of better times, but she knew she couldn't stay there, out in the open as she was. That was stupid. She had to get her head together, start thinking clearly. Start thinking like Alice.

Reaching up, Samantha grabbed hold of the handle for the rear driver's side door. Unlocked—a stroke of good fortune. Ever so slowly, she creaked it open just enough to squeeze herself through and close the door without making a sound.

She lay face down on the floor of the Jeep, below the back of the front seats. The rain hammering against the roof that she had felt overbearing on their drive was now peculiarly calming, and quiet in comparison to the sound of nature punishing the surrounding landscape.

Her phone was in the center console, the red notification light blinking its warning that the battery charge was nearly depleted. She grabbed the phone and hit the power button. The screen came immediately to life. Her eyes snapped to the battery indicator—2% remaining.

Just enough to make one call.

The background wallpaper was a family photo taken alongside a calm river. They all wore life jackets; Samantha, her mother and father, and her sister. The sky behind them held a touch of gray, but it was otherwise an idyllic snapshot.

She had little time to waste. Her fingers trembled as she dialed 9-1-1 for the first time in her life.

The call was answered immediately. "Nine-one-one.

What's your emergency?" the voice of the operator asked.

Samantha opened her mouth to speak, but only a crack of dry air came out.

"Hello?"

Samantha cleared her throat. She could only muster a whisper. "Help me. Please, you have to help me."

"What is your emergency? Are you hurt?"

"Yes. But my friends…"

"Are you currently in a safe location?"

Samantha chanced a look out the front window, glancing toward the house. "I don't know. I'm safe for now, I think."

"Are you able to move?"

"Yes. I…"

"Ma'am, what is the nature of your injury?"

"I can't… I can't take a deep breath. I fell. On a rock." Samantha sucked in quick breaths in rapid succession. The conversation had her heart pounding. Safety was on the other end of the phone, ready to come and rescue her and her friends. Knowing she would have to wait for that moment to come, that it would not be instantaneous, was the hardest part.

"What is your current location?"

"I'm … at a house. White farmhouse. About twenty minutes from the highway."

"Which highway?"

Samantha's words quivered with emotion. "I don't know." She hadn't been paying attention. She had been too concerned with the storm they were driving into. It had terrified her. The warmth of the morning sunlight had faded fast as a blanket of black, cumulonimbus cloud cover unfolded on the horizon, as if heralding a malevolent tempest before her.

"Are you alone?" the operator asked.

"I'm … my friends were … taken into a house at gunpoint."

"Did you say at gunpoint?"

"Yes, they were taken against their will. You have to send help." Samantha couldn't believe the words coming out of her mouth or the situation she had found herself in. She'd had nightmares that felt more real.

The operator's voice had vanished without warning.

The phone screen went black. The battery was dead.

A thousand thoughts flooded Samantha's mind. She should have texted someone instead. She could have sent ten texts instead of making one phone call. But who would she have texted? Her parents? They couldn't help her from the other side of the country, but they would at least know where she was and what had happened. They would be as helpless as she was. Any help they could lend would be preceded by an eternity of waiting. Waiting for help to arrive. Waiting as they wondered why she wasn't responding on her phone. Waiting and more waiting.

She wanted to scream, but she couldn't find the energy. The pain was terrible already, and she knew she was unable to handle much more.

Then she remembered Julia's painkillers. Samantha found them on the back seat and popped the cap open. She had no idea how many to take. Her knowledge of pharmaceutical drugs was essentially non-existent, but she knew these had to have plenty of strength for what Julia went through. This scared Samantha, but at this point, she just wanted the pain to go away.

Her thoughts went to her sister; Alice wouldn't have

been scared. She was fearless. Independent. Adventurous. Outgoing. Alice was a free spirit, but Samantha often found herself unable to muster the courage to be more like her. For Alice, it was natural. For Samantha, it was an ongoing struggle. When encountered with a situation where the opportunity presented itself, Samantha turned away and crawled back into her comfort zone. She was simply a different person.

One, it was decided. She threw the painkiller in her mouth and crunched the pill between her teeth like candy, burning with the pungent taste of chalk and medicine. She was searching for a drink to wash it down with when she heard the wind clap shut the front screen door of the house.

All color drained from Samantha's face when she peeked out the window.

The man with the shotgun stepped off the porch and aimed his stride toward the Jeep.

FOUR

THE HINGES OF THE JEEP'S driver's door creaked open in a whine of metal against old metal. Rain rushed in sideways, tormented by the fierce winds howling in the nearby fields. The vehicle rocked to one side as the man sat in the seat. The door slammed, shutting out the din of nature's fury. A sudden silence hung in the stagnant air like words unspoken.

From her spot on the floor behind him, Samantha heard the man set the shotgun on the passenger seat. She had grabbed Bobby's hoodie and thrown it over herself in a hurried effort to remain hidden. It was all she could think of at a moment's notice. Pressed flat against the floor of the vehicle, her heart beat louder than the thunder. She was certain the man could hear it.

The man slid the key into the ignition and started the Jeep. It was an older model, Ted's first car that he bought with his own money. The muffler was louder than it should be. The engine worked hard, strained by years of effort. News radio came through the speakers at a low volume, but loud enough for Samantha to comprehend.

It was a welcome buffer to mask her labored breathing and the pounding in her chest. Or maybe it would be a distraction, and take her focus away from remaining as silent as possible.

She didn't know what to think. She kept her eyes open under the hoodie, staring at the worn upholstered floor. Her eyes would not close. She had to see what was happening to her, even if it was nothing.

The man shifted into drive and let his foot off the brake. The next thing Samantha knew, they were rocking against the movement of the tires over the unpaved dirt path before the house. She couldn't see any window from her vantage point. She stopped herself from wondering where they were going. Not something she wanted to dwell on.

What had happened to her friends inside? She'd heard no discharge from the shotgun, or any firearm; heard no scream, no cry, no struggle from within the walls of the stranger's home. They must still be okay, she reasoned. Had he let them go? Ted would surely have come looking for her the first chance he got.

No, they were still held captive. They must be. Locked in a spare room, perhaps, or chained in the basement awaiting whatever punishment the homeowner was envisioning for their unwelcome intrusion.

Samantha tried to stifle a shiver and failed. *Don't move. Don't make a sound. Don't breathe.* She couldn't breathe. *Do nothing. Say nothing. You've remained hidden this long; you can't give yourself away now.*

The ride was rough, driving hot knives into Samantha's side with every bump. It took everything she had not to cry aloud. One whimper would be enough to put an end to this cat-and-mouse charade. Staying hidden was a struggle, one that Samantha was not prepared to endure. But she did her best and hoped it would be enough.

Suddenly, forfeit didn't seem like such a bad idea. Just

one little noise and she could be with her friends again, indoors, away from the wind and the rain, safe from the storm. Giving up would be easy. A groan, a whine, anything that meant she no longer had to be out on her own.

The shotgun slid and fell onto the floor in front of the passenger seat. The man paid no mind and kept driving. Samantha heard the clatter of the weapon falling. She was facing the other way and could not see, but she felt certain the gun had fallen out of the man's reach. No way could she get to it before he did, or before he caught her arm as it shot out in a feeble attempt.

But she knew this was an opportunity. She could reach up and lock her hands around his neck, choke him before they got too far from the house. He was too strong. She could dig her fingernails into his eyes, claw at his face, tear at his ears, do *something*. An opportunity for her to subdue this man was not likely to come again. She knew it would be an even greater struggle than remaining silent and immobile. She would have to fight this man, but she could not conceive of any scenario where she would come out the victor.

She remembered the screwdriver tucked away in her back pocket, but an even more dangerous weapon she possessed was the element of surprise. Before the man knew what happened, he could have a cold metal spike buried in his neck.

Samantha couldn't believe what thoughts were circling around inside her brain. *That's murder. What the hell are you thinking?* She'd be sent to jail, probably for life. Self-defense wouldn't fly. Maybe her friends weren't in any trouble at all, and she would have the intentional killing of an innocent man on her conscience.

That was not something she could deal with. Wild, absurd thoughts Samantha couldn't in a trillion years believe she would entertain. This was crazy. The whole situation was crazy—hiding on the floor of the Jeep with her friends held hostage in a random stranger's house halfway across the country during the worst storm she had ever experienced.

Samantha nearly laughed aloud. Not in a trillion years could this have happened.

The news radio program ended, switching to a weather advisory.

"And we hope everyone is staying safe this afternoon, as the National Weather Service has upgraded the status of this storm into a Tornado Outbreak Warning. One tornado was spotted not long ago, and more are expected to touch down later in the day and into this evening, as one system has unexpectedly merged with another over the Kansas-Nebraska border, resulting in a supercell. It's very dangerous out there, folks, so stay indoors, and away from windows. If you have a storm shelter, it is advised that you take immediate action to—"

The man switched the radio off.

Samantha held her breath as the Jeep slowed to a stop. They did not travel very far. Down the dirt road, she guessed, back toward the main road. Make the Jeep look abandoned as its occupants hastened to take shelter.

Maybe, instead, he moved it deeper into his property, away from the main road where no passersby could spot it. Anyone in search of Ted's vehicle would be on their way and leave the man to his own devices without another thought on the matter, never knowing what was unfolding inside the home.

The man cut the engine and removed the key. The

door opened in a rush and he was out, shotgun in hand.

At the slam of the door, Samantha exhaled. She hadn't realized she was holding her breath. The painkiller must have started taking effect. Her side still felt quite sore, but tolerable at this point. She drew a few slow breaths, which came easier than before.

Another door creaked open beyond the confines of the Jeep. Samantha was too frightened to look up just yet. The man could be coming back, for any number of reasons. Coming back for her was the one she felt most likely. She cursed herself again. *Don't be stupid. He doesn't know you're here. You're safe.*

Nobody was ever angrier with Samantha than she was with herself. She should have done something to help her friends, but all she could do was stay on the floor and cower. She did nothing when she could have taken a chance, and now that chance was gone.

Samantha never regretted anything she had ever done, only the chances that came and went without her taking action. Great times missed out on, words unsaid, potential friends and relationships that hadn't escaped her imagination of what could have been. She dreamed as big as anyone, but could not find the courage to wake up and see those dreams become reality.

Now was not the time for dreaming.

Samantha knew it was not safe to remain in the Jeep. She raised her head ever so slowly to survey her surroundings. A sigh of relief eased her to a degree; the man had parked the vehicle behind the house, out of sight from the dirt path, and far enough away from the main road that no passing motorists would spot it.

The rickety garage that she had been hiding in, little more than a worn old shack, was at the opposite end of the home.

It was a hazard to try to get back there unseen, not that Samantha wanted to be there to begin with, but she knew the man had little reason to venture out that way. There was nothing of use or value inside; apart from the old Chevy that she guessed didn't even run. She had found no keys, and the layers of accumulated dust and grime on the windows were an indication that fixing it up was not a high priority on the owner's to-do list.

Samantha's options were limited by the severe weather. The attempted call for help was a failure. She was too far from any decent form of shelter, other than the house in which her friends were being held captive. Their drive down the main road earlier in the afternoon was all but void of other homes, businesses, even passing vehicles.

Samantha was, quite literally, stuck in the middle of nowhere.

But the storm was getting worse, inconsiderate of her plight or that of her friends. She had to make a choice, and make it soon.

FIVE

THE AIR INSIDE THE OLD farmhouse was thick with humidity. All the windows were shut and locked tight, curtains drawn. The glow of the old tube television failed to light the room properly as an early dusk settled above the storm.

For the moment, it was quiet, an unsettling quiet that gave no hint of the events that had transpired before Ted and his friends' arrival.

In the kitchen, a man lay dead. In the adjacent dining room, a woman stood bound and gagged and still unconscious. The man who had just moments ago stepped onto the front porch carried a shotgun, but Ted spotted no spent shells on the floor or any sign of a blast on any of the walls or furniture. His view of the kitchen, however, was obscured.

Bobby wrestled against his bindings. The zip ties were too tight, digging into his flesh from the effort. "See if you can get your hands loose, Ted."

"I can't."

"You didn't even try!"

Ted shot a quiet shush at Bobby. "Keep your voice down," he whispered.

Bobby gave up for the moment, exasperation flooding in. He spoke in a lower tone. "Do you want to just sit here and wait to see what he does next? I don't."

Julia called in a whisper from where she sat on the steps across the room. "Sorry. He was watching me do it."

"It's not your fault, Julia," said Ted. He faced Bobby. "What I don't want to do is piss him off. Let's wait for him to calm down a bit before we do anything we might regret."

Bobby exhaled his frustration. "Julia, can you get free?"

Julia's eyes dropped to the floor and she gave a shake of her head. "No chance. Guy must be a god damn Boy Scout."

"Eagle Scout." The voice came from the direction of the back door.

The man let the door close behind him and he carried the shotgun into the living room. He failed to acknowledge the woman tied to the large cabinet as he passed. Ted recognized the gesture—or lack of one—as intentional.

Once again, the room fell into silence.

Moments passed without a word, without anyone moving. The man then collapsed onto the couch in an exhausted slump, shotgun across his lap. His clothes were dappled with fresh raindrops, hair windblown and unkempt. Dark stains and splatters of what could be blood soiled the lower area of his pant legs and the ends of his rolled-up shirt sleeves.

Ted guessed this was the longest day in this man's life, a day that showed no signs of ending any time soon. It had been a long day for all and it was not yet evening, though it looked as if midnight was fast approaching—a far cry from the warm, golden sunshine of that morning.

They had been on the road for several hours following

an early breakfast at a hole-in-the-wall near the motel they had occupied the night before. Who knew how long they had been on that same lonely stretch of highway? Nobody was counting the hours. Except maybe Samantha. It was something she'd do.

Samantha was her usual introverted self the entire trip, never hinting at what was going on in her mind at any given time. She was a closed book to all but immediate family and close friends like Ted. Julia she had met once before, the previous year's 4th of July cookout at Ted's place, but she didn't know Bobby from Adam.

Ted wondered where she might be. Safe, that's all he wished for. In his current situation, Ted couldn't help anyone. Not even himself. The cable ties were strangling his wrists. There was no wiggle room. He could feel the blood flow to his hands restricted. The tips of his fingers tingled. Sitting like this for too long needed to be avoided, Ted realized. An hour or two at the most, that was his best guess before it became an emergency.

Time was a commodity growing more precious as each minute dripped away, and the storm was getting worse. How long it would take before their captor came to his senses and thought of a resolution that did not involve any more deaths was a mystery. Ted's concern over the man toting the shotgun grew and would not stop growing.

Perhaps he would not find his bearings today. Or tomorrow. Or ever. He might kill them all, the woman in the next room, and then himself, leaving only Samantha to find the bodies of her friends in the crimson aftermath, stranded in this secluded farmhouse in whatever state they were in. Kansas? It didn't matter.

"Excuse me," Ted said in an assuaging voice.

The man turned only his head to meet Ted's eyes, and for the first time, Ted got a good look at the man who had taken them captive.

A blank face stared back at him, bereft of any emotion. Dark eyes too fatigued to hold on to despair, anger, sadness, or remorse. The man was now a blank slate, his life taken from him. He gave no reply apart from the derelict stare.

"Excuse me," Ted said again. "My name is Ted Downing. These are my friends, Bobby Welliver and Julia Thisbe. We were run off the road by a tornado and were only looking for shelter."

Bobby's face swelled with barely contained rage. If his hands were unbound, he would have strangled Ted himself for saying their names aloud.

Ted had second thoughts about what he'd just said, wondering if it was as smart as he had assumed. Humanize the nameless faces and it might help the man care enough to let them go; that was the best plan he could formulate.

Julia did not react one way or another. Her head had been turned away from the man since he sat down on the couch. It wasn't fear; Julia was not afraid of anything as far as Ted knew. She hated being powerless, being a victim.

The man blinked several times, as if straining to process Ted's words. "Well, I'm sorry," the man replied. "You showed up at the wrong place at the wrong time. Just like him…" He followed with a gesture toward the kitchen and the unmoving stranger sprawled face-down on the cold, tile floor.

Ted considered how to reply. "We… We don't know anything about that."

"We mind our own business," Bobby blurted out. He

ensured his message was clear.

Ted looked at Bobby cross. They were walking a fine line, and Bobby's natural reaction to conflict—agitation and confrontation—would not do them any good here.

"Call me Michael." The man took a long breath before he continued. "Now tell me about yourself, Ted."

Ted cleared his throat and composed his words carefully. "We're on a trip to Oregon. My family owns a place near Rockaway Beach."

"You have a lot of luggage for three people."

The trunk of the Jeep was packed near to the ceiling; with Samantha's belongings added to the pile there were more than enough bags for the three of them.

"We're staying for two weeks," Ted lied. They had two weeks to make it back to Pittsburgh before the summer came to a close. Work and classes awaited them. The idea was to spend one week at Ted's aunt's property and spend the second week driving back home. They would stop along the way at whatever cities or landmarks looked interesting enough to warrant more than a passing glance.

This was not one of those landmarks. The nearest major city was miles upon miles away. The name of the nearest town? No clue.

Michael's vacant eyes found Julia across the living room, arms still bound within the railing of the staircase. She hadn't moved since he sat down. "What's wrong with her?"

Bobby spoke up before anyone else could answer. "She has a bad back."

"Is that so? Are you in pain, Julie?"

"*Julia*. With an A," Bobby spat in a voice laced with venom. Ted swung a covert kick at Bobby's calf while

Michael's eyes were averted, followed with a silent "Shut up!"

Michael stood. Set the shotgun aside on the couch. "Hey, Julia with an A. I asked if you're hurt."

Bobby tensed where he sat, but heeded Ted's request. Michael's boot steps knocked heavily against the hardwood floor as he crossed to where Julia sat. Every step was a beat that skipped in the hearts of the two immobile friends tied to the radiator.

Michael loomed over Julia like a predator pitying its wounded prey. He glared down at the back of her head, turned away from the face of her captor, just the way she liked it.

"What's wrong?" Michael asked in a neutral tone.

Julia said and did nothing.

Michael bumped his boot against her foot ever so gently. "You don't have to look at me, but I want an answer."

Bobby's heart beat like a wild beast chained in a cage too small, ready to pounce but without the ability. Forced to watch. Rage contained only for now.

Julia turned her head to look upon Michael's face for the first time. Hard eyes greeted him, a look of cold steel that would neither bend nor break. Even at her lowest points, Julia possessed a strength few would ever need to channel in the whole of their lifetime. She had a will of iron, battle-tested. "I'm fine," was all she said, her voice plain.

"That's good," said Michael.

His hands went to his pockets and the next thing Ted saw was the glimmer of something in Michael's fingers, a snap of metal as the box-cutter opened in his grip.

Bobby's voice caught in the back of his throat. Ted stared a wide-eyed stare. It happened too quickly for his mind to keep up. His only thought was that Julia was dead. He was about to see his friend murdered before him, hear the thud of her body colliding with the floor, the dull thump of rag doll limbs meeting hardwood.

But the only sound was that of the plastic cable tie as it landed at Julia's feet.

Her hands were free.

Now she found herself unable to look away from Michael, bewildered at her unannounced freedom.

Michael slipped the box-cutter into his shirt pocket and locked his gaze upon her. "I need your help."

SIX

Growing up on the East Coast, Samantha had never seen this type of weather in person. She was never further west than Auburn Hills, Michigan; a family road trip to a place called The Palace to see the Pistons play the Timberwolves. It had to be ten years ago.

But for how little sports tended to interest her, it was a fond memory. Alice was the sports nut who always rooted for the local teams. Since there was no NBA team in Pittsburgh, she chose Minnesota for a reason Samantha did not know.

As excited as Samantha was about the prospect of traveling further west to Oregon, it took a week of Ted's insistence before she agreed to tag along. Traveling without her sister by her side was a foreign concept, an intimidating step she had not imagined she would have to take, at least not at this point in her life.

Her world had been thrown into turmoil once Alice was gone. Samantha had felt as though a piece of herself was gone, too.

The basement was warm and dry. Everything Samantha's fingers touched carried a thin layer of dust, and the chill had returned when the bare soles of her feet touched the concrete floor.

It took her two full minutes to get the basement door open without making a sound. Hanging on the latch was a brown padlock, rusted to the core, which no longer closed. Samantha had discarded it and eased the weather-beaten door open just enough for her to sneak around.

Her ribs felt okay, even after pressing them against the doorjamb as she squeezed her way into the basement. Sore, but okay. Tolerable. She valued that painkiller more than anything.

There was little sound from upstairs. A footfall every few minutes; the muffled voice of an indeterminate speaker here and there. No struggle or commotion. Everything appeared calm. It brought Samantha some repose, for which she was thankful.

She groped through the darkness, feeling her way, the black robbing her of sight. Her fingertips found what she judged to be the chain of a bulb hanging from the ceiling, but she chose not to pull. She couldn't chance the light being seen if the man happened to leave the house again. The darkness must be her ally for now.

A voracious reader, accounts of weather in Tornado Alley were described to Samantha in books many times, though she assumed the words had been embellished for dramatic effect. Now, having been run off the road by a funnel cloud that had touched down in the path of their Jeep, she understood the truth of those descriptions.

The storm had transformed into a cauldron that was threatening to erupt at any second. Samantha concluded that she made the right choice, getting out of the elements and into shelter, even if that meant sneaking into the heart of the lion's den.

Cobwebs hung at face-height every five feet. Samantha wiped her grimy palms against her face every time she felt the brush of something against her cheek, and again when she simply thought she'd felt something.

This was dangerous, she knew. *Get a grip. Stop imagining things. It's all in your head.*

Alone in her head was somewhere Samantha did not want to be. She spent more time in there than anywhere else, and knew how easy it was to convince herself that things were worse than they were.

Things were already bad enough. She wondered if coming inside was the right move. One scream, one yelp, one peep, and she would be caught. There was nowhere to run.

Several places to hide, however.

She questioned her own thought process. *Is that your best idea … hide? Keep hiding until you're found out? That won't help anybody. Get real.*

What else was there to do? Barging up the stairs was out of the question. She didn't even know where the stairs were located. She couldn't see her hand in front of her face. The steps could be right in front of her or twenty feet behind. Maybe there were no steps going upstairs at all. *How stupid was that? Get a hold of yourself!*

Truth be told, Samantha had no plan. Get out of the rain and wind and flying debris—that was it. Was this any better than the Jeep? Probably not. Neither was ideal. She'd have to make do with what she had, which was very little.

She felt hunger settling in. She remembered that her last meal had been early in the morning—silver dollar pancakes with a drizzle of real maple syrup and a side of the best seasoned home fries she had ever tasted, finished off with four slices of wheat toast with just the right amount of butter and cinnamon, and washed down with a tall glass of pure-pressed orange juice. They had chosen the most nondescript eatery they could find, knowing that's where you're most likely to discover great, homemade food.

The meal was so satisfying they skipped lunch and agreed on an early dinner instead. As soon as they passed this storm. At the time, it felt wiser to attempt to outrun the clouds looming overhead than to stop and wait for safer skies to shine through.

A regrettable choice.

It was a fact Samantha was learning to come to grips with. All that was happening was real. This living nightmare was not something she could wake up from. It had to pass, like the storm that churned and threw the landscape into turmoil beyond the walls and windows of the home. And Samantha understood that, in time, it *would* pass.

Time. It had never been on Samantha's side. Every day seemed shorter than the last. Missing hours left days feeling empty. One empty day after another. Something was missing, something Samantha did not possess to plug the hole and slow the vacuum of passing minutes that had defined too many days in recent memory.

The last day she was with Alice was a day much like this one. The sun had risen early, lending the day an early warmth. It wasn't officially summer, but the promise of season's change was strong.

They were on the river before nine o'clock, and the day was only getting warmer. Not a cloud dressed the sky. The blue was striking, a big, blank canvas on which to paint random shapes in vague patterns of white. It was

Samantha's favorite childhood game. Sitting on the grass with her big sister, gazing up at the sky on a clear summer day; there was no better way to pass the time.

First, Samantha had seen the head and neck of a giraffe. Alice had argued that it looked more shark-like, with a wisp of a dorsal fin and the grey color to match.

Samantha had not noticed the color.

She pondered it only for a moment before the sun retreated behind another bank of clouds that reminded her of butterfly wings, darkly drawn against a deeper shade of blue. A shadow in the sky.

Samantha had not looked upon the sky this trip. She kept her eyes cast down, locked on the landscape, on the passing bush or tree or field or car, never hovering above the horizon.

She liked it this way, paying attention to the sights of everywhere they went, not letting the details pass by. From sleepy, rustic hamlets to the busy steel and glass metropolis of well-known cities and all they happened across in-between, her eyes were more open than they had ever been.

It wasn't until Bobby had commented on the alarming storm clouds that were fast emerging from below the horizon of an endless stretch of Midwestern highway that she felt compelled to see for herself.

Smoke-like. Anvil-shaped.

A boom of thunder sounded from above a distant town. Whoever lived nearby must have retreated to their cellars, as well … if there was anyone else living nearby.

There could be a group of homes less than a mile away for all Samantha knew. A family just beyond this farmland, even, huddled in a cinderblock corner below their ancient dwelling, praying the roof over their heads and their very livelihood would not get sucked into the sky and scattered in a mile-wide haphazard clutter of the broken homes of other families.

Another thought jumped into Samantha's head—*What if the man upstairs decides to come down into the basement?* It's the safest place in the house in the event of a tornado, Samantha had heard a long time ago. The news radio in the Jeep had said something of a tornado outbreak warning, so the possibility of another twister landing in the vicinity seemed very real.

If this structure was threatened, he would have to come down for safety reasons and bring the others with him.

Then Samantha would be found.

The only other option was for her to leave. Beyond the battered basement door could be the help she and her friends needed. If that was a fact, it was stupid not to go.

But what if it wasn't true? What if the closest friendly place was a handful of miles in an unknown direction, and Samantha wasted valuable minutes—hours—running away from sanctuary instead of toward it? It felt somewhat stupid to abandon her safe harbor and bank on such an uncertainty.

Another shiver crawled up the damp goose bumps on Samantha's legs, giving her a shudder that clung cold to her spine, a chill that she couldn't seem to shake.

Her feet would be torn up, trampling through debris-strewn fields with no footwear. It was enough of a challenge to navigate the unswept cellar floor without feeling a small stone or piece of wood or what she hoped was not a nail digging into her heels with each blind step.

For the moment, Samantha chose to take that over the notion of finding herself stranded in the eye of the storm, lost without aid, especially when the effects of her painkiller decided to wear off.

Samantha shook her head, brushed wayward strands of hair away from her face. *No. This is just like you. Always taking the easy way out. Doing nothing when you have the chance to act. Stop being afraid. Stop worrying. Do something, Samantha!*

She turned herself around in spite of the dark, one foot at a time, careful not to lose her sense of direction, and found her fingers on the handle of the wooden door leading outside.

The sounds emanating from beyond were almost enough to change her mind.

No. You have to do this. You have to find help.

She would make it to the road, avoiding windows as she passed alongside the home. From there, she'd continue onto the main road and walk until she found someone—anyone. Another home, a passing motorist, whoever was willing to take a moment and listen.

Samantha closed her eyes and inhaled a slow breath that calmed her nerves just enough to convince herself she was ready.

Then the basement light flicked on.

SEVEN

"If you try to run, I'm going to shoot you. If you get away, I'm going to shoot your friends. Is that clear?"

Julia nodded. Her lips were drawn tight to ensure she didn't mouth off from reflex. Bad habits were hard to break.

Michael returned the nod. "Remember, I'm trusting you by letting you free, so I need you to show me some trust in return. Don't do anything stupid. If we get this done, we can all sit down and think of how to send you on your way. Okay?"

Another nod.

"Let me hear it."

"Okay." Her single word hung between them like a spider's web. Then, "What do you want me to do?"

Michael lifted a finger in the direction of the kitchen.

The look of disgust was plain on Julia's face. Another reflex. When she didn't like something, she let people know. The reaction was often an unintentional one, but never regretted.

"I'll give you gloves. So you don't get any on your hands. We have to be smart about this. The less you get on yourself, the better."

Julia stole a glance at Bobby, who sat unmoving, rigid as a creature who had just suffered a paralyzing sting. Ted's eyes hung on him with the most concentrated look of anticipation Julia had ever seen.

Shortly after they first started dating, Bobby had body-slammed some dude on their high school's cafeteria floor for not holding a door open for Julia. A bit of an extreme reaction, she thought at the time, but that's the way he knew to keep his girl safe. Then he helped the poor guy up and invited him to sit at their table.

Julia had dogs that were not half as protective as Bobby had always been to her, or as warm-hearted. He would do anything for her, which is why Ted wore such a look of concern. It was clear that Michael did not want to deal with any more unpredictable events this day.

Julia gave her fiancé a subtle nod, assuring him that she was fine with the duty Michael assigned to her. It wasn't like she had much of a choice.

"There are gloves under the sink. Be careful where you step."

Michael flicked the switch for the overhead light. The scene was thrown into high-contrast white, like the room of an autopsy you'd see on one of those crime shows playing on every cable station that wasn't showing reality TV at the moment. Julia expected it to appear much worse that it was, to be more like the shows she had seen so many times.

Instead there was just a man she had never known who appeared to be sleeping peacefully on the floor, surrounded by tiles stained red, tiles that would likely never see their natural white again.

Exhaling, Julia did as she was asked. She kept close to the counter while navigating around the body. She snapped the rubber dishwashing gloves on, an absurd rubber-duck yellow, that only fit over her engagement stone after some effort.

As morbid a situation as it was, she had to chuckle at what she was about to do, at the luck of Michael picking the least squeamish of the bunch to aid him in the cleanup, at the day in general.

"Towels are in the second drawer, left of the sink," Michael announced from his position as sentry at the doorway. He received a double-take from Julia when she saw the shotgun in his bloodstained hands, as if it had materialized there. She did not hear him move for it or return to his post.

Shotgun held at ease toward the floor, Michael kept his shoulders perpendicular to the door frame, allowing one eye to watch the radiator in the living room and the other to supervise the kitchen.

Julia grabbed all the towels she saw and threw them one at a time into the dark pool that encircled the center of the room, watching the blood draw into the cotton of each towel like a liquid parasite, turning pastel orange and cornflower blue alike a deep, wet shade of almost black. The overhead light lent a cardinal tint.

Blood was much darker in reality, Julia thought. TV always got that wrong.

With the last towel, she wiped down the edge of the countertop that struck the fatal blow. The blood was still fairly wet, but wiping it up meant smearing it all over the place, as blood tended to behave.

She guessed that the act had taken place not long before their unsuspected arrival, based on the condition of the man at her feet and the blood that now saturated the towel in her gloved hands, dripping.

Julia discarded the towel into the pile with the others, haloing the dead victim. "This is a bad idea, you know." Her words were spoken at the wall, but directed to Michael.

"It's a bad idea to keep talking. Just work."

Julia wiped the tip of her nose with a clean part of her gloved wrist. "Just sayin'… This all looks involuntary to me."

Her words gave Michael momentary pause. He thought for a moment and then said, "There's a bucket under the sink. Soap and warm water. I can't have any left on the counter."

Julia shrugged her shoulders at him and went for the bucket. She filled it as instructed without a word passing between them. Until Michael broke the silence.

"What are you, some kind of expert?"

Julia sloshed a sponge around in the bucket and threw Michael a glance before she slapped it on the red counter and scrubbed. "Only at watching TV," she said.

Michael shook his head as a smirk drew across his lips. "Just think about getting that clean. I'll worry about everything else."

"Okay," Julia said contentedly.

Her initial shock was wearing away quicker than the stain on the counter's edge. She felt freedom in her hands being cut loose, albeit to complete a rather messy chore that she played no part in creating. Still, she'd rather scrub the house ceiling to floor, upstairs and down, before spending one more minute tied up and unable to do anything. She had to move, be active, as much as her body would allow before the pain settled in.

At her feet grew a pink puddle that merged with the clump of soaked towels. The floor was a disaster, but the edge of the counter was clean. No visible evidence remained.

Julia swabbed her brow with her bare forearm. "Not much more I can do with him in the way," she said, indicating the anonymous body with her foot.

Michael studied her work from his spot in the doorway. "We'll get him out of the way and get you a mop." And he entered the kitchen.

"Only pair I found." Julia started to remove the gloves, but Michael raised a hand to halt her.

"I'll be fine." His hands were already stained, most likely from the act itself. He seemed resigned with his incrimination, accepting of his actions rather than running from them.

Julia didn't understand if this was good or bad for her and her friends. She felt the best course of action was to play along, do as she was asked, keep moving forward, past this moment and into the next, moving ever forward to safety and release. It appeared to be the only chance they had. Samantha would be long gone at this point, off to who knew where. If there was help to be found, it would not arrive for several hours at the least, with Samantha being on foot and the weather making matters worse. And she didn't seem to be the most confident in the face of trouble, either—or when things were going well, for that matter. It was something Julia could not count on.

Michael stepped up to the body, leaning the shotgun against the kitchen wall as he passed. "Grab the legs," he said and crouched to take hold of the dead man under his arms.

Julia hesitated. "What are you doing?"

"*We* are going to get rid of the rest of the evidence."

"I can't."

Michael stood. "Yes, you can. You've helped me this much already. Grab the legs and help me move him."

"No, I can't. I'm not supposed to lift anything over fifteen pounds."

"Why not?"

"I have a bad back. We've been telling you this whole time."

Michael huffed his frustration. A cold glare penetrated Julia, one that spoke of a violent reaction from Michael if she was lying. He didn't have to say a word for the message to be delivered.

Julia said nothing in return. It would be a mistake to open her mouth, regardless of what was said. Michael seemed in no mood for smart-ass remarks, of which Julia held an extensive repertoire.

It had been eighteen months since she fell. She had gone down the double black diamond dozens of times before, so there was no reason to assume this run would be any different. Bobby was already at the bottom waiting for her so they could pack up and drive back to Kim and Jeff's house and call it a day.

The next thing she remembered was waking up in a hospital bed to find she had seven cracked vertebrae and a bruised spinal cord, with ligament damage to her right knee.

"Lucky" was the word the doctors had used, much more often than she cared to hear. Julia did not feel so lucky, particularly after hearing other words thrown around like "freak accident", "life flight", and "back surgery".

Bedridden, hooked up to machines with tubes running out of her arms, she felt imprisoned for a crime she did not commit. She had asked the nurse how long she would be stuck there.

The nurse's reply angered Julia to the point that she did not speak to anyone for two whole days, not even her own boyfriend of six years, and did not walk again for two months. In that time, her friend Kim had competed in the Olympic trials and made the U.S. Alpine team.

Julia would never ski again.

After a moment of thought, Michael spoke his idea aloud. "I'll hold him up; you just make sure the legs don't get in the way."

Better than being lashed to the railing again, Julia decided. Concern over aiding and abetting in the cover-up of a killing never crossed her mind. Bobby and Ted would agree that she was forced beyond her will at gunpoint. The word of three against one; the culprit stood no chance.

Perhaps that was why he acted unperturbed in his decisions. A man operating solely on impulse. Julia had seen enough TV crime drama to think she had him figured out, if there was any truth to the procedures and diagnoses they presented. But the one thing she couldn't speculate on was what his plan was for her and the others once this evidence was wiped away.

She doubted Michael had thought that far ahead. The way he moved was sure, his behavior deliberate. The perception was that he still possessed all of his faculties, but what was lurking beneath the calm demeanor was anybody's guess. A man doesn't commit manslaughter, voluntary or otherwise, and remain mentally unaffected for long.

It was the smart move, Julia thought as she stood there, deliberating, as Michael waited for her to help move the body. Keep assisting him and he may maintain this current disposition toward her and Bobby and Ted.

Put up a fight and…

Julia bent at the knees carefully and grabbed hold of the corpse's legs. "Where are we going?" she asked.

Michael motioned with a jerk of his head toward the nearest door. "Into the basement."

EIGHT

LIGHT BATHED THE BASEMENT, casting out the darkness.

Samantha's initial thought was lightning, but she understood quickly how wrong she was. A single, dim bulb spilled a yellow glow ten feet from where she stood by the door that led out to the back yard.

At first frozen in place, her shock dropped away in an instant and she dove for cover behind the side of the washing machine next to her. She barely caught sight of where the steps that led up to the first floor were located, but she saw enough to put an object between her and whoever was about to descend those steep stairs.

A flash. Lightning this time. A nearby grumble of thunder unfolded soon after.

Samantha's eyes darted side to side, finally free of the choking blackness. With no way of knowing how soon the light would go out, she wasted no time surveying the area.

It was one large room with round, wooden, load-bearing pillars every so many feet. Plenty of clutter to hide among—or stumble upon. Samantha counted her blessings for the miracle of her not making a sound when wading through the area robbed of vision.

But now she could see, and what she saw was very little

from her vantage point. She wasn't stupid or brave enough to risk a closer look with footsteps and voices falling in from the open door at the top of the steps.

One of the voices was unmistakably Julia's. She loved to talk, and always found something to talk about. Her sarcasm was spared for nobody; Samantha thought she must have said something to piss-off the man with the shotgun, and that he was throwing her down the cellar to keep her out of sight, down in the dark where she would no longer be a nuisance.

Samantha believed she had seen a stone doorway at the opposite end of the basement, but couldn't be certain. She imagined rusted chains and shackles hanging from the cold walls, and the bones of previous victims piled neatly in the cobwebbed corner.

It was a hard image to shake. There must have been a thousand stories of psychotic killers living in seclusion, in off-the-beaten-path farmhouses not so different from the one above her head; closest neighbor a twenty-minute drive away, far beyond earshot where screams go unheard. Passersby would never suspect a cache of bodies entombed under the front porch steps, or the perverted acts of deviance committed beyond those drawn bedroom curtains.

Shut up, Samantha. Shut up!

She slammed her eyes shut tight. *Stop thinking like that. Get a grip. You need to stay focused.*

Stay focused.

Stay.

Focused.

Her eyes flew open with a sudden pang of terror. The presence of a man standing over her felt tangible, immediate.

Nobody was there.

Again, she forced herself not to look away, to see everything that was going on around her, even if it was nothing. Her imagination was far more terrifying than whatever was likely to actually be happening.

The voices on the stairs grew louder, but words remained indecipherable. Footfalls danced a random pattern at the top of the steps, drunkenly heavy. Two sets of feet—Julia and the man who presumably lived there, Samantha guessed. Then the creak of the hundred-year-old boards of the top step as weight was put upon them.

Then the next step groaned.

Then the next.

The descent was curiously slow and deliberate. It brought to Samantha's mind memories of playing hide and seek, hiding in a closet or under her bed in her childhood home. Alice liked playing tricks on her little sister, learning where she was hidden then creeping around the room in a plodding shuffle, sure to make obvious noise in an attempt to scare Samantha out from her hiding place. It worked more often than not, and when it didn't, Alice would jump behind her and give a startling shout that would send Samantha scampering from the room.

More than a decade later, she still hated that game.

She heard labored breathing drifting down the stairs. Shadows capered in the light on the wall. The duo landed on the concrete floor, set down the large silhouette they had been carrying, and paused to catch their breath. Julia's shape laid its palms flat against the wall, head down, unkempt hair hanging free.

Whatever it was they had brought down the steps, it was heavy. Julia sucked in deep breaths, stood upright and brushed the hair from her face.

Why the man had chosen Julia for such a chore made no sense to Samantha. She was no doubt still recovering from her injuries. Most of the trip was spent with Julia laid across the back seats with Bobby's leg as a pillow. The upright seated position did her no favors.

Samantha recalled a conversation as they were driving late one night through Indiana, where Ted expressed his concern to Bobby about how taxing the long ride would be for Julia, who was sound asleep at the time. Bobby blew the question off. He knew Julia better than anyone and was confident that she would have no problem. More importantly, he knew Julia was confident. There was nothing Ted or Bobby could say that would keep her from coming along.

Judging only by their two brief encounters in the year since their first meeting, Samantha saw enough in Julia to know that they couldn't be more different. Julia had the body of a life-long athlete and the features of a movie star, always smiling as though she was walking a red carpet, approaching every situation with enthusiasm. She was not afraid of a challenge; in fact, she welcomed them. She was comfortable in her own skin, confident.

Samantha was huddled in a damp corner out of sight while Julia was assisting this man. There was no fear in Julia.

"Let's go," the man's shadow said.

"Give me a minute, okay?"

"One. Then we work."

The silhouette swung something off its shoulder, and Samantha recognized the shape and sound of the shotgun in the man's grip. She prayed she would never have to hear it another way.

Curiously, no other sounds accompanied the scene. The two stood in silence. Nobody followed them down the steps. In fact, no footsteps from overhead were heard. No creaking of floorboards, no conversation.

It was as if nobody was upstairs at all.

Ted and Bobby must be tied up somewhere, bound and gagged and waiting their turn to be thrown down in the dungeon at the back of basement. The man was too smart, too paranoid, too in control to leave them up to their own devices.

"Alright," Julia said, and lifted her share of the cargo. Together, they carried it away from the wash of light and toward where Samantha had seen the stone doorway.

Their footfalls echoed off the concrete, retreating in the direction of the unknown room where they grew silent, as if Julia and the man had stopped dead in their tracks. The sound of their voices felt distant.

All was quiet. Quiet to the point that Samantha was unsure if the voices she heard were real or were now a product of her imagination.

She refused to move from her hiding spot behind the washing machine. Or was it a dryer? *Why are you thinking about that? It doesn't matter. Stay focused, Samantha.*

The light from the bulb still spilled from overhead. Samantha wondered how long before her world would be in total blackness once again.

The basement fell into a fragile stillness. Where there had been sights in the shadows playing on the wall and noises as her friend and the stranger descended the steps, there was now only a silent snapshot, inviting Samantha to creep out and explore what had been hidden from her moments before.

No. She was not moving. She remained seated on the floor and hugged her knees tight to her chest. One move would give her away. One noise and not only would she be in trouble, but so would Julia as well. And what of Ted and Bobby?

Samantha was trapped in this corner with no way out. No way of helping Julia. No chance of making a break for the steps and dashing up to the first floor. No likelihood that any such action would benefit her or her friends.

She couldn't even be sure that Ted and Bobby were on the first floor. No time to go looking through the house for them. If it was Samantha who had to lock somebody up, she figured she would put them in a room on the second floor, or in the attic, where jumping out the window was dangerous and out of the question. Fewer escape options that way.

Not the safest place in this weather, though; that was the basement. Samantha didn't feel any safer knowing that, certainly not with the man down here toting his shotgun, waiting to fire it at a sudden moment's notice.

Or maybe that was his plan—bring everyone down one at a time to wait out the storm where it's safe. Practically no windows down there. No fear of glass or debris flying around. Few high shelves meant little danger of falling objects.

Visions of the man chaining Julia to the wall stuck in Samantha's head like a splinter.

The house shuddered, raining thin streams of dust from between the boards of the ceiling overhead. The wind howled and the hanging blub swung its light in a gentle circle, turning the frozen scene into a maddening fun-house as the light danced from wall to wall, object to object, calming ever so slowly.

Samantha wished she had worn a watch. She always just looked at her phone. But her phone was dead and sitting in the Jeep outside. There were no clocks on the walls anywhere that she could see. How long had they been in that back room? Five minutes or an hour, Samantha couldn't guess. Her sense of time was sitting dead, outside in that Jeep; her sense of place had been gone from the moment the Jeep left Pittsburgh.

She heard little conversation coming from the back room. Either they were not speaking often, or not speaking very loud. It must be hard, she figured, to strike up a conversation with the man holding you hostage. Julia could do it, no doubt, but the gift of gab was not a trait Samantha had ever possessed.

Sitting on that filthy floor, cold and hungry, wet and sore, tired and alone, Samantha wished she had someone to talk to. She didn't like the sound of her own voice, hated it, in fact, but the feeling of complete isolation that enshrouded her, the silence that it brought, was a far worse sound. Even if the other person did all the talking, that would be good enough. Someone had to tell her that everything was going to be okay, tell her that her friends would be okay, tell her that this would all be over soon, and that everyone could go home.

Home. Forget the vacation.

Samantha hadn't thought of Oregon all day, she realized. Her focus was always on the trip, not the destination. She enjoyed sitting in the Jeep for those long stretches more than she'd expected to. Sitting in the front passenger seat, window rolled down, bare feet resting on the side mirror, head back and eyes closed as the passing breeze slipped between her toes and danced in her hair. The conversation was a soothing sound. Voices of friends, their laughter, their jokes. Samantha joined in on occasion, typically only when prompted to. Listening was good enough for her. Just being there was enough.

Now her feet ached, bruised and blistered. Mud had dried between the cracks of her toes. The curls of her hair were matted flat to her head, ending in a senseless confusion of knots that fell haphazardly over her shoulders. Her clothes were as filthy as the floor beneath her, perhaps more so, stained the color of dirt. A swelling ache was returning to her side, every breath more difficult than the one before.

Worst of all, there was nobody there with her, nobody to talk to, nobody to listen to. There was a voice inside her that couldn't come out. The sounds of those oblivious to her presence provided her only company. And it had to remain that way.

Samantha lowered her head to her knees in silence.

NINE

BOBBY COULDN'T UNDERSTAND HOW TED could sit there, body still as the corpse that was just carried down the basement steps, eyes fixed on the antique television set in all its standard-definition glory. There wasn't even any sound. The reporter's lips moved, but the only information they gathered was from the ticker scrolling across the bottom of the screen, and the occasional footage of someone's home ripped apart board by board and strewn evenly across half a mile of brown dirt.

It scarcely felt like what they saw was civilization. Who would want to live there? A few of the shots looked more like what Bobby had envisioned man's first attempted colonization of Mars would look like if ravaged by a natural disaster. A few standing structures, dozens more demolished, nothing around them except fields and dirt.

A vast expanse of emptiness.

As they had passed deeper into God's country on their trip, it had become more and more obvious why, when settlers went west, they hadn't stopped along the way; America's heartland had nothing to provide, apart from false promises of a better life.

Bobby's wrists throbbed against the pressure of the thick

cable ties that held his hands firmly in place. It didn't help that he had not stopped struggling against them ever since Michael retreated to the kitchen to keep a watchful eye on Julia. Now that they were down in the basement out of the way was as good a time as any to find a way to get free.

The ties were a thick grade, not to be broken easily. A wrestler in high school, Bobby had plenty of upper body strength, but the weird position of his arms behind him while seated afforded no leverage. The ties held strong.

"Cut that out, man. You're making too much noise," Ted whispered.

"What do you want me to do, Ted?" Bobby's whisper was considerably louder, born of the frustration of not being able to walk down the basement steps, punch this Michael guy out, and lead his girl to safety.

Ted kept his eyes on the TV. "Don't do anything."

"What do you mean don't do anything? Julia's down there, and I don't like that. I don't like that for one second."

"I don't like it either, okay? But we have to be smart about this."

Bobby could feel the agitation simmering behind Ted's words. Maybe it was the right thing, to be smart, think things through, find the best solution so nobody got hurt. But that was Ted's skill, not Bobby's, and they did not share the same definition of what the best solution was.

Bobby didn't think analytically. To him, there was no grand design. There was no right thing to do, or wrong approach, as long as they came to the solution—that's what mattered. They didn't have time to weigh every opportunity and pick and choose the best course of action, compare and contrast the positive and negative outcomes and try to avoid what, in theory, might not work.

In Bobby's mind, the only thing that didn't work was not acting. They had to act, not think. Thinking wouldn't free his hands from his bindings, or bring Julia back up the stairs unharmed. They could think about it all they wanted when they were back on the road, driving far away from this hellhole of a place.

Bobby turned to Ted with a quiet voice. "Where's Sam?"

Dammit. Samantha. He'd been told that she never liked being called Sam. He slipped up two or three times when addressing her directly, but she never corrected him. It was just easier to say than Samantha.

Nevertheless, Ted hadn't said her name since he stepped through the front door. He shook his head and returned to watching the muted weather reports.

She probably ran for help, Bobby assumed. It would take a while, given that the last sign of life they saw was a general store twenty miles back. Maybe she was hiding. She seemed timid, always on edge. Ted didn't like talking about it, so they sat quietly, staring at the ticker on the screen as it counted up the storm's death toll.

Bobby had sensed that Samantha was troubled by something since she first sat down in the Jeep. He had a way of understanding people without them saying a word, just by their actions, movements, and subtle behaviors. He used it to his advantage on the wrestling mat, tried to size up his opponents to use their weaknesses against them, then do all he could to get them locked in that one hold, that one position they kept shying away from more than any other.

But he couldn't put his finger on Samantha. She held

her cards close to the vest. Bobby asked Ted about it the first time they stopped to stretch their legs at a convenience mart somewhere in western Ohio. Ted didn't say much. Perhaps he was thinking Bobby was trying to snoop and spy on her private life, but it was just his way of getting to know her better.

When they first heard the weather report of the storm system directly in their path, he noticed Samantha was on high alert. For what, Bobby had no idea. He'd asked Ted again the next time they stopped. Samantha stayed in the vehicle with Julia while the men grabbed some extra bottles of water. None of them anticipated the strength of the heat that day.

Ted, once again, said very little. Bobby had dropped the secret that Julia was afraid of ducks, in hopes that it would spur Ted into giving another hint at what was troubling Samantha. Ted only laughed at the thought of the girl who wasn't afraid of anything running from a harmless little duckling.

Bobby sucked in a deep breath and exhaled. *They've been down in the basement too long. What is he doing to her? It should not take this long to hide the body, at least temporarily.* He wanted them back upstairs. He had to see Julia was safe. Every moment she was away turned a wheel in his head, cranking tauter against the tension with each passing minute.

When Julia was laid up in the hospital following her skiing accident, Bobby read her coursework to her. She wanted to stay on top of the lessons so as to not come back to school and find herself facing the insurmountable task of learning everything she missed in a short amount of time. One more year and she would graduate with her class. The idea of lagging behind was out of the question, broken back or not. She had two dreams in life. The first was to be an Olympic athlete and win a gold medal, which she now knew would never come true. The second was to be a guidance counselor, leading wayward kids on to the right path and helping them follow their own dreams.

Bobby recalled a passage in one of her psychology texts, something about the effects of emotion on the human brain. He couldn't remember the words verbatim, only something about how the way the mind behaves when experiencing feelings of deep love for another is strikingly similar to the way the mind behaves when stricken with mental illness—particularly insanity. The message had always stuck with him.

Maybe Ted was right, as he usually was. If Michael was no longer able to think rationally, they were in a lot more danger than it seemed. He was alone with Julia. One wrong word out of her mouth could trigger something inside him, some primal, animalistic tendency to strike back, much in the same way the dead man's skull struck the edge of the counter before he slumped to the floor and expired in his own blood.

"So, then what do we do?" Bobby asked.

The light of the TV reflected in Ted's pupils. "Give me a minute to think."

"We've been sitting here for an hour already."

"I know. I've kept track."

"So?"

Ted held a distant gaze on the images that played on the TV. "It said that in 1974, a hundred and forty-eight tornadoes hit the United States in less than eighteen hours. In 1999, one hundred and fifty-two in less than a week's time."

It might as well have been a foreign language to Bobby. "Ted, listen to me. We can't just sit here watching TV all day."

Ted glanced over to him, seemingly free from the entrancement of the news reports. "I don't know what happened to Samantha," he said. "She's in a lot of danger, but this guy can't know about her, no matter what."

"For sure."

"If he finds out we're hiding anything from him, it's going to be bad for everyone."

"I know, I agree, but we can't help her if we're tied to this god damn radiator."

Ted flashed a look that urged quieter conversation.

Bobby lowered his voice to a conspiratorial whisper. "Okay. I'm sorry. I know. Listen, the longer we allow this guy to do whatever he wants, the more … unstrung he's gonna get."

"What are you saying?"

"I'm saying we have to act while he's still somewhat calm. He's trusting us enough to let Julia free."

Ted chewed this over. "He picked the one he thought he could control the easiest—physically control. When he found out she was hurt, he could have chosen you or me, but he didn't. The security of control was more important to him than getting the job done. He doesn't trust us; he trusts himself to be able to handle her."

"Then he'll be more willing to take risks and chances as he becomes more confident, right?"

"Perhaps."

Bobby shifted his weight, moved his body as much as he could to look at Ted face to face, to reason with him. "Hiding a body is a pretty big risk. Covering up all the evidence is a pretty big risk."

"Letting us go is a pretty big risk," Ted said.

"That's not what I'm saying—Jesus Christ, Ted. *We're* evidence."

Ted appeared deep in thought. There was a long silence before he spoke. "Whatever we do, we have to be smart about it. Show that we trust him, that he has a reason to trust us."

"The sooner, the better," Bobby said.

The rain fell more intensely with every passing minute. A flash lit up the sky beyond the curtained windows.

Ted nodded. "I agree. It's not safe here."

Bobby felt a hint of relief. Convincing Ted was just the first step, but he could see the faintest hint of light at the end of their very dark tunnel. "So, what now?"

"I think I might have an idea," said Ted. "Bathroom breaks."

A smile crept across Bobby's face. "That's it, you beautiful bastard! I knew you and that idea-filled brain of yours would come through."

"Hang on, it's not that easy."

"Why not? When you gotta go, you gotta go."

"He may not trust us enough just yet. This is likely to be our only chance. If we don't do it exactly right…" He finished with a shake of his head.

This was just like Ted. Come up with a brilliant idea then shoot it down after thinking about it too much. Bobby's smile went away. He felt the pressure building in his forearms, in his wrists, his throbbing hands, his blood-swelled fingers. "We have to do *something*," he said through clenched teeth.

"We will. Just wait for the right moment."

Bobby snapped hard eyes to Ted. "No, we can't wait any longer. We're only giving him more time to think about how to get rid of us. Don't you see that? And the quicker we get free, the quicker we can find Samantha."

The name weighed heavily on Ted's mind, Bobby knew. Could see it in his eyes. He wouldn't take a chance for himself, but for Samantha…

"If he wanted us dead, he would have done it by now," Ted said.

"He's working up the courage. And don't you think the thought never crossed his mind."

"Perhaps. But I don't want to trigger anything that could cause his thoughts to drift in that direction."

Ted's way of thinking was clear. They couldn't help Samantha if they were dead. It made sense, but Michael keeping them alive did not. Why didn't he pull the trigger before? He needed help disposing of the first victim. But after that?

Maybe he didn't want to make a mess of his house. Wait for the storm to pass then march them outside one at a time to a nice crop of tall grass and do the deed there. It would be easier to hide a body in the middle of nowhere than in his own home.

"I don't get it, Ted. You'd rather sit here and think of excuses," Bobby said. "I don't know about you, but I'm not giving up. If you want to sit here all day like her—"

With a tilt of his head, Bobby pointed to the woman in the adjacent room, standing with her hands bound behind her, cable ties fastened taut to the doors of an oversize china cabinet, gagged with a white cloth.

Ted turned his head to look.

Wide eyes stared back through the dark. Feral eyes. The unconscious woman had awoken.

Ted and Bobby froze. A stunned silence hit the room.

They had no idea how long she had been listening.

TEN

THE LANTERN'S LED LIGHT WAS enough to illuminate the small room. Michael set it on the ground next to the body. Four cinderblock walls and the one doorway. No windows. No decorations. No furniture. No floor, either. Only dirt.

Julia felt the softness under her feet. "What is this?" she asked.

"She wanted a back porch, so we built a back porch. Something about 'irregular soil', so we had to build a foundation." Michael didn't say her name, but Julia knew he meant his wife.

They had dropped the body from the kitchen near the center of the room. She knew what was coming next. Michael tossed a shovel to her feet. Julia looked at it then up to Michael.

He held the shotgun at his hip and aimed vaguely in Julia's direction. "Well, what are you waiting for?"

Julia had to suppress a laugh. This was ridiculous. Was she really just asked to do this? Perspiration dripped from her brow from the effort of carrying the dead weight down from the kitchen. Her back felt stiffer than usual, but not painful. Not yet. She knew the results of more physical exertion. It would not be pleasant.

"You've gotta be kidding me, right?" Julia still made no move to pick up the shovel. She thought maybe this was a test, to see how far Michael could push her, to see how much leeway he had with them.

"I'm not kidding. This needs to happen." Michael was startlingly relaxed, his gestures persuasive, not threatening; his words collected, not delivered with any hint of anger.

Julia pointed to the ceiling. "Why don't you have Bobby or Ted help? I won't be very good at this."

"I have faith in you."

"I have seven fractured vertebrae in me, and they don't like it when I bend over, alright?" There was indignation behind her voice. It was not a topic she enjoyed bringing up.

Michael's reaction said that he had not quite understood the severity of her injury. They never did. It was a look she thought she'd be used to by now, and wished that she was, but the dismay in their eyes, the way they always tried to mask their revulsion with pity… Her bones may have healed, but that wound would always be there.

"How did that happen?"

Julia had not expected Michael to ask. "Skiing," she said, and found herself staring at the dirt floor, the shovel before her, the running shoes on her feet that she could no longer run in.

"Must have been some fall."

Julia swallowed the lump in her throat. "That's what I'm told." She turned her gloved hands toward the light of the lantern. Little rivers of red had run down the length of the rubber, onto the bare flesh of her forearms and crawled their way to her elbows.

Michael pointed the shotgun to the shovel. "Just do what you can."

It was hard to keep playing along, doing what she was asked, but Julia reached for the shovel regardless, struck it into the ground and lifted away the first clump of earth. She had to do something, at least a little bit. She wasn't ready to push back and see how much leeway she had over him. Refusing would draw that anger out of Michael, and that was the last thing she wanted to happen. As long as he stayed cool and collected, he would be easier to reason with, and they would still have a chance at leaving this place sooner than never.

One by one, she lifted away the little scoops of earth. She toiled without words between them. Michael leaned against the wall near the doorway, the only way in or out of the room. All the while Julia's hands worked the shovel, digging and lifting and dropping and repeating, Michael's hands held a firm grasp on the stock and barrel of the shotgun. He shifted his stance on occasion, refitted his fingers around the weapon like a nervous tick.

A sense came to Julia's mind, a feeling that Michael did not feel comfortable being so close to her while she held the shovel. A tool, but a weapon if it had to be, like the sharp, unprotected edge of a granite counter top, used to break open a human skull.

It was a silly thought for her to entertain, turning the shovel on the more heavily-armed guardian of this unfinished back room crypt. Doing so would only find her in the same shallow grave with the man for whom she was digging. There couldn't be any intention of doing other than what she was asked.

Julia was never one to back down from a fight, nor or give in to submission without exercising a valiant struggle of her own. Before her fall, and after a few drinks, she would find herself in misguided attempts to pin Bobby's shoulders down to the floor. Her two-time state champion boyfriend would best her every time, even when he was considerably more drunk than she was, though he would later claim that Julia put up a better fight than half of the opponents he'd faced. The difference was confidence. Where the young men stepped onto the mat with their fear still lurking in the back of their minds, Julia attacked with such assuredness, as if this was the time she knew, damn near clairvoyantly, that she would take Bobby down and pin his shoulders for victory. And even in defeat, she rose up and said with a wry smile, "Next time."

Those days were gone.

Much of her upper-body strength was left on the ski slope that fateful afternoon, replaced with a weakness that was foreign to her. It was rare that she found herself truly challenged, but to struggle with simple, everyday tasks like getting out of bed, standing up under her own power, walking… A fire was lit that day, deep in a lonely, dark place she never knew existed inside her. Every helping hand, every word of encouragement, every wheelchair and cane and physical therapist and rehab session, every act of weakness found her blood pumping harder, racing through her veins, in and out of her heart so fast that she had to just curl up her fists and draw in a deep breath. She felt the oxygen filling her lungs, fanning the kindling of that fire to give it the life she no longer had.

Those days were mostly gone, as well, by virtue of avoiding what she knew she could not do. Her confidence had turned to ash in the hot coals of that smoldering fire.

She was recovering, she knew, getting stronger every day. But even now, feeling the shovel's weight in her hands, filled with curiously heavy lumps of dirt, Julia felt something inside her simmering to a boil. The need to draw in a deep breath and fan the flames growing at a pace quicker than the size of the hole she was digging. It shouldn't be this hard. The hole should be three times the size by now.

Julia drove the shovel's blade into the dirt so it stood on its own. She yanked off the rubber dishwashing gloves and threw them aside with a force that caused Michael to stand at attention. She felt his eyes hanging on her, heard his bloodstained fingers adjusting their sweaty grip on the shotgun. Her hands curled into tight balls, and Julia stood upright, arching her back, stretching the stiffness away.

One hand wiped the sweat from her face; the other grabbed the shovel out of the dirt. She wrapped both fists around the long, wooden handle of the digging tool, and with a deep inhalation of the musty cellar air, she went back to work.

Michael's glare still hung on her like the wash of light spilling from the LED lantern. She operated in a machine-like rhythm, which seemed more efficient than if she stopped for any length of time. She wasn't feeling any pain at the moment, just stiffness. Periodically, she spotted Michael's eyes averted toward the ceiling, his concentration not on the sound of the metal hitting dirt, but on the rooms above. He listened like this for only brief moments at a time then his focus was back on Julia. Scoop by scoop, the grave widened, deepening with the passing minutes.

"And you said you wouldn't be any good at this," Michael finally said. They were the first words either one had spoken in the past twenty minutes. In fact, there were no voices heard at all. Bobby and Ted were equally as mute, and Samantha … who knew what was going on with her. Julia's first thought was that the house had fallen into silent mourning for the anonymous stranger at her feet. The wind and rain without played their dirge in lower tones, as if Mother Nature herself paused to pay respect.

Julia planted the shovel and leaned with both hands against it. She met Michael's eyes, hidden in the shadows cast by his brow; the reflected light her only indication that he had any eyes at all in this moment. Her only reply was a shrug of her shoulders.

"Not too much more to go. We can finish it now or later. Your choice."

Julia wasn't sure she heard the words right. He was giving her an option, something he hadn't given them prior to this moment. It was a change, she noted. He certainly wasn't the taskmaster she had expected him to be while she was digging the grave. Not at all. He simply stood back and watched. She hoped this was a change for the better.

"Let's get it over with," she said between breaths. She took the shovel once again and went back to the task. She was feeling good, much better than expected. Physical therapy had been paying off. She'd be stiff as a board by the evening, though. Motel mattresses were cheaper than the dirt she was shoveling and, more often than not, twice as scummy.

A stark realization rushed at her all of a sudden: they were not sleeping in that farmhouse that night. Michael would never allow that. No chance. It was much of a risk for him to leave the three of them alone for any length of time. The only reason he was leaving Bobby and Ted alone upstairs, Julia knew, was because he had her. He had the upper hand. If they got loose while she was down here and ran off, or didn't, or did anything other than tie one another back up, she would be dead. They would never take that risk.

Julia estimated that the probability of Michael letting them go was frighteningly low. Someone else was going to die that night. The understanding fell heavily on her every thought. No matter how hard she tried to shake it, there it was, with roots dug deep in her mind. Things like this don't just take care of themselves. People aren't just let go. Witnesses like her and Bobby and Ted, who had seen what they'd seen, aren't freed with a handshake deal. Julia knew, deep in her heart, that this was just one of those universal truths in life.

But at the same time, Michael didn't seem to her like a cold-blooded murderer, either. Just a guy who made a mistake. Everyone acted out of anger once in their life. Doesn't matter how saintly you are. Everyone has snapped at a moment of stress, done something they cannot undo, said words that can't be unsaid, had one of those human moments everyone seems to have in spite of their best efforts.

Everyone.

With every scoop of the shovel, Julia's back grew tauter, like someone was turning a crank, twisting and stretching every muscle and tendon and ligament. She could tolerate an uncomfortable feeling for a while, but this was something new. She hadn't worked herself to this point yet, and she wasn't enjoying this new territory.

The thought of spiking the shovel's blade in the dirt and calling it a night crossed her path several times, but the motor inside insisted she keep at it, better judgment be damned.

No sooner did she convince herself that she was too close to stop now than a cry from above bled through the walls and floor. The shovel stopped in her hands out of sheer reflex. She made no sound, no movement. Michael snapped to high alert, weapon on Julia.

Again the voice sounded, echoing throughout the house, feeling its way through the rooms overhead and down into the cavernous basement. Inside the stone walls of the small back room, it resonated in ghostly tones. Julia's first thought was that the old farmhouse was most definitely haunted.

Michael shifted his weight toward the door. "Don't move from that spot. I'll hear you if you do." Before Julia could say a word in reply, he was gone.

Julia kept her mud-drenched running shoes planted in the soil. Moving didn't cross her mind. Not for one second. All she wanted was to rest—to allow herself to rest. She was always her harshest critic, her own greatest motivator. It was a blessing and a curse. The times she allowed herself a moment's respite were seldom.

Michael's footsteps crept farther away from the back room at a snail's pace. He was moving toward the stairs, Julia thought, getting close to the door to hear the source of the sound. It wasn't Bobby, that was for sure. Ted? Unlikely. The cry was higher in pitch, more feminine, but dry and ragged, like a dog's bark after it had been disturbed from a long sleep. Could it have been Samantha?

The hoarse voice cried out once more. Louder, clearer. This time, a word was distinguishable, one single word.

A name…

"Michael!"

The footsteps darted back to the room and Michael appeared in the doorway. "Let's go. Come on, over there." He made a vague gesture toward the main area of the basement, and Julia lifted her ruined shoes from their spot in the dirt and left the body of the unknown man alone next to his final resting place.

"There, against the pole. Face-first. Wrap your arms around it," Michael said with a quick shake of his elbow in the direction of one of the support beams. Julia did as she was bid, though not without fighting off a smile at how ridiculous it was to hug a wooden pole in the basement of a man she never met before this day.

She heard the sound of a shotgun being set down on the washing machine. Her peripheral vision saw Michael unbuttoning his shirt, little more than a rag of dirt and blood now, and tossing it aside.

Michael picked up the shotgun, now in his undershirt and still wearing his filthy pants and boots. "Up the stairs, one at a time. Move." There was an edge to his command, a hint of urgency. This wasn't good, Julia thought. Just moments before, his mind seemed at ease, almost tranquil. This shout of his name jolted him back to that state of unrest she saw on the porch when he had opened the front door and ordered her inside earlier that afternoon.

That passed, and this will pass too, Julia reminded herself. But following her up the stairs was a hovering sense of dread, a presence that lingered in the back of her mind. Of what, she did not know. She turned her thoughts away, toward the hope that she was walking away from the deepest, darkest recesses of this home and all the secrets they hid, burying them forever, away from the grave and toward the release of her and Bobby and Ted and even Samantha.

Each step was more difficult the than last. Her back began to ache, and her hands were shaking. But why? Her hands never shook. Her palms were never sweaty, either.

Julia then realized she had never been more terrified in her entire life.

ELEVEN

THE WOMAN WORKED THE GAG from her mouth with only her tongue and jaw after considerable effort. Ted watched it all happen, his eyes glued to the awakened victim.

She had heard every word he exchanged with Bobby, no question about it. Their secret was out, and now the woman was calling for her husband to spill him the information. It was her only hope of securing her release, Ted thought. Turn against the other prisoners. Show that she's not one of us, not in this with us.

In truth, she was not like Ted or Bobby. Her role went much deeper. A participant, not merely a spectator. Where Ted had driven his friends to this house in a mad dash to take shelter, this woman was the very reason anyone was tied up at all. Ted understood that his presence was merely a surface nuisance, and if he wanted to secure his own release and that of Bobby and Julia, it would need to remain that way.

Footsteps hurried up the basement stairs, two pair. Ted snapped a glance to Bobby. "Don't say a god damn word. Not one." An edge of authority backed his command. Ted had that in him, when he chose to show it. He didn't like being the leader often. It wasn't an avoidance of initiative; he found it fascinating to watch how those around him behaved.

This, however, was a situation that demanded his natural capacity for leadership. He knew how Bobby was going to behave; Bobby was never a passive person.

Ted felt the air retreating from the room when Michael entered, escorting Julia to her spot at the railing of the steps leading to the second floor. Bobby's stress was palpable, but he remained motionless and without words as Michael secured another of his thick cable ties to Julia's wrists and bound her arms behind her, entwined in the posts of the baluster.

The woman had stopped calling for her husband. Fear was the reason; Ted saw it in her eyes, in the lines around her mouth, in the way she didn't move. It was sheer terror, he realized. A look he had never seen before, and didn't want to see again. Pure, unmitigated terror. It consumed every part of her, inside and out. It filled the house like a contagious disease, infecting the minds of everyone inside.

Everyone except Michael.

He crossed the floor and stepped into the woman's view. She lifted her eyes behind a mask of dangling hair, dark and dripping with perspiration, and showed him a look of the most sincere regret. It had no effect. Ted noticed the woman's gaze, locked on her husband's emotionless face, noticed the shotgun held firm in the man's grip. Sheer willpower kept her eyes from averting toward the weapon. She strained to look away from the weapon, seeing it but not seeing it.

"Why did you do it?" Michael asked.

Tears fell in clean streaks down the wife's dirty cheeks. "I... I don't know, Michael. Please..."

"Answer the question."

The woman struggled for words. She stood a breath

away from sobbing outright. "I don't know. It was a mistake. I made a mistake and I don't know what to say."

"There's nothing to say. It's done. And it can't be undone," Michael said. His words came out in a rehearsed calm. He turned his back to the woman and began a slow pace around the living room. "The mistake wasn't the act, was it? You were okay with that part. You thought about it, planned it, and put that plan into motion. You *wanted* to do it."

"I didn't want this, Michael—"

He turned his face to her. "You didn't want to get *caught*. That's what you didn't want. Someone was going to get hurt, you knew this. Right from the start, you knew it would hurt someone—you, or me."

The woman turned her head away, eyes shut, refusing to meet the accusations face to face. Ted didn't think of saying a word. Even Bobby was silent. It was too weird, too uncomfortable to be a part of, yet there the three of them sat.

Bobby exchanged a comforting look with Julia from across the room. There was pain on her face, physical pain. She blocked it out as best she could, but both Bobby and Ted knew it was there.

"You could have told me if you were unhappy," Michael continued, "but that would hurt. You'd rather hide your true feelings behind closed doors and save that hurt for me to find out all on my own. Well, guess what, Carla? You got what you wanted."

Carla wept; her only answer to her guilt. Michael dropped onto the couch, threw his head back, and covered his face with his soiled hands. "In my own house. In the *kitchen*. Couldn't even make it upstairs," he said. He spoke to nobody. To himself.

Ted watched Michael's chest rising and falling with measured breaths, as if under a heavy burden. Storm winds gained velocity beyond the farmhouse as the rainfall resumed.

Wherever Samantha was at this time, Ted hoped—no, he *knew*—that it had to be better than this. He was thankful she didn't have to bear witness to this family quarrel against her will. The whole thing was ridiculous. To him, at least. Ted tried to put himself in Michael's shoes, understand what he was going through, the emotions he was feeling.

That was impossible. Gaining an understanding of Michael's state of mind would be of unquestionable value at this time—knowing the right thing to say, the right actions to take at the right time to find the quickest and best resolution—but what did Ted have in his own life that could stand in comparison to this?

Not one thing.

This level of betrayal was not something Ted had experienced. He doubted that he'd lived long enough to get to that point, to feel years' worth of love and commitment and trust snuffed out like a candle in one unanticipated moment. Of course, he had no idea how far back the love of Carla and Michael went, or how many times a sudden breeze made their flame dance on its wick, stumble, spill some wax down the side, only to stand up tall once again. Perhaps their light was never at rest, flickering instead of burning in a bright, solid glow.

Whatever the impetus was that brought these two people to this point, Ted could only speculate. But what good would that do? As Michael had said, it was done. And couldn't be undone.

A sudden tone invaded the stillness of the farmhouse, brief but prominent. Ted recognized the sound immediately as the text tone on his cell phone.

Michael raised his head when the noise had concluded. His eyes landed on the three phones laid out on the coffee table in front of him, drawn to the notification light blinking its guilt on Ted's phone.

There was a moment of indecision. Would Michael pick up the phone? Ted already knew the answer before Michael leaned forward and picked the phone up. Curiosity was a powerful drug, one that was now eating away at Ted from the inside. Who sent the message, what it was about, what it would mean for him and his friends? Questions with fearful answers.

Please don't be from Samantha. Please don't be from Samantha. The words repeated over and over again in Ted's head, a mantra with no end. *Please don't be from Samantha.* She was smarter than that. She wouldn't have contacted him this way, no. She was smarter than that. *Please don't be from Samantha.*

The light of the screen cast a yellow glow on the distressed features of Michael's face. Tired eyes reflected the message as he read. Either the text was long, or Michael chose to deliberate on each word. His mask of no emotion failed to change.

When the screen went dark, Michael set the phone in its place on the coffee table and leaned back as he was before. Then his head tilted back and his eyelids shut. Everyone else in the room exchanged eye contact, pondering the next moment.

But the next moment did not come. Michael remained seated, resting with his shotgun across his lap, still as a statue, apart from his slowly rising and falling chest, like that of a sleeping beast not to be woken. There was no aggression, no more words of accusation, no inquiry concerning the nature of the text message.

Only rest.

Ted wondered how anyone could rest at a time like this, even for a moment. But he was not in control, he realized. Michael held command over everyone in the house, so much so that not a single word was uttered during this interval. If anyone had thought about speaking, they were too apprehensive to voice whatever was on their mind. Even Bobby kept his thoughts unspoken. His concern was for Julia, and the growing anguish that accompanied her every movement, her every breath.

Julia was in pain.

It was known to Ted that what could create such a reaction in a person as strong-willed as Julia Thisbe was not a situation to take lightly. Though not an outright emergency, she needed a resting place of her own. Crouching with her hands bound behind her to the railing of the stairs would not suffice.

No sooner did Ted finish the thought than Bobby cleared his throat, presumably in an attempt to spur Michael from his catatonic state.

There was no response.

"Excuse me," Bobby said.

This time, Michael lifted his head just far enough to find Bobby in his field of view. "What?" Michael's voice was dry.

"She needs to lie down," Bobby answered with a tilt of his head in Julia's direction. "And painkillers. Please."

Michael's eyes shifted to the area where Julia sat. Her

expression was traced with distress. "I don't have any painkillers," he said.

"They're in the Jeep."

Looking back and forth between Bobby and Julia, Michael filled his lungs with a breath that seemed to have no end, and then he left the room, exiting through the rear of the home.

As the back door creaked open with a whine, Ted leaned forward and craned his neck to get a first-hand glimpse of the weather outside. Rain spilled from the sky, an endless supply of water that was drenching the already soaked back yard and field beyond. Thousands of drops plummeted into the surface of the pond, making splashes that reminded Ted of a volley of arrows. And the wind howled.

An early night was upon them.

Michael left the storm door open, letting the screen door slap closed. Ted listened to the intense hiss of nature's tumult.

Carla turned an unhinged glare to Ted, her voice a touch louder than the storm. "You kids need to get the hell out of here."

TWELVE

AT THE SOUND OF THE door being shut atop the stairs, Samantha flung the filthy shirt away. It had landed on top of her head, unbeknownst to the man with the shotgun. Thankfully.

Her heart was in her throat and her breath in her belly. As hard as she tried, her hands wouldn't stop shaking. She wrapped her arms around her body, but that only made her shoulders spasm and her spine shiver in concert.

Samantha knew what a panic attack was; she had felt it a handful of times before. This was not it. This was something new, something different. This was fear achieving a physical state. This was worse. She was one tear away from a complete breakdown.

Then it stopped, as quickly as it began.

A warm feeling washed over her, warmer than the sun that had shined that afternoon. This, too, was new. The uncertainty of what and why and how was nearly as alarming as the attack itself. She flattened the soles of her feet against the cold floor, hoping to absorb some of the concrete's chill.

What she felt was cold. And wet? Samantha opened her eyes and looked to her feet. She hadn't even realized her eyes were closed. It took a moment for everything to register as the flood of emotions faded and her body performed a natural reset of chemical and hormone levels. She had read that in a book after the first panic attack all those years ago.

It was senior year of high school, one month before graduation. Third period English—her favorite subject. The feeling, a form of stress she had never felt before, came first to her right arm and then to her right leg. Her mind raced with crazed thoughts. Heart attack? Stroke? Her heart beat so hard it seemed as if it was trying to escape her body. The pen she held between her hands snapped, spilling blue ink on her brand new pink blouse, but Samantha was only thinking how thankful she was for having a reason to leave the room. She had darted out of class and found herself in the girls' restroom, sitting in a stall, door locked, hands grasping two fistfuls of her strawberry-blonde locks.

The source of whatever had happened, which she later grudgingly defined to be a panic attack, remained shrouded in secrecy, even to this day, as she now sat on the concrete floor watching the water pool around her feet.

Before she knew it, she was standing, moving away from the flow of water. The light at the bottom of the basement steps hung bright enough that Samantha had to raise a hand to shield her face. She told herself that it would take a moment to adjust, that it had happened before and that she was going to be okay. She was always okay before. Just one more minute and she would be okay again.

Nobody knew of this affliction that had plagued her for the last five years, not her parents, not her best friend Ted, not even Alice.

If one person was going to know, it would have been

her big sis, but the onrush of water that had swallowed Alice's canoe took with it any chance Samantha would have to speak with her sister again.

And now the rainfall spilled in from the few tiny basement windows, each half the size of a sheet of paper, seeping through the seal around the panes and collecting on the floor. As the pooling water encroached on her spot beside the washing machine, Samantha eased away, into the heart of the basement, under the wash of light.

Out in the open where she could be seen.

She brushed twisted locks of hair from her face, and her hand came back wearing a smear of wet red. Fingers probed for the source of the wound, and she found it near the top of her scalp. Small and insignificant, though it bled like something far greater. Only now did Samantha feel the dull throb of pain in the area of the gash. *Where did that come from?*

Looking up, she saw nothing that would have caused her harm. Only a network of dusty old webs that hung innocently from the boards and supports overhead. The only thing she could think of was the shirt. It had fallen on top of her in perfect form, like a burial shroud, only this one was plaid instead of white, reeking of sweat and stained with someone else's blood.

Samantha tiptoed around the water, the balls of her feet finding only the dry spots. *Don't step in the water. Stay dry.*

Something in her head, a prodding thorn of certainty, was telling her she wasn't safe unless she was dry. In a sense, it was rational. She'd entered the basement of the old farmhouse to escape the swirling winds and downpour of rain. She wanted to be dry and warm, but each dip of her toes in the muddying water chilled the marrow of her bones and served as a stark reminder that her day was far from done. She felt the dampness of her clothes clinging to her chilled skin, as that of a corpse.

Using the washer for support, Samantha leaned over the puddle and pulled the man's shirt up from the floor. It dripped, half sodden from the water that streamed down the wall, but even so, it hung curiously heavy in her hand.

Samantha located the source of the weight and found it to be the breast pocket. She slipped two fingers in and they touched cold metal, hard and unforgiving. No doubt the object that scratched her head. She withdrew her hand along with the object.

Samantha now held a box cutter.

It was the kind that folds open to nearly double its length to reveal a triangle-shaped blade that likely hadn't been replaced in the past decade. Dull as it was, it could be used, Samantha thought.

But what if he came back down looking for it? If it wasn't in the pocket of the shirt that now lay crumpled in a puddle against the corner of the basement walls, he would know something was up. Or maybe he'd assume it had fallen under the washing machine when he discarded the shirt. Maybe he wouldn't come back downstairs at all. But the light had been left on. He and Julia had retreated up the stairs in a bit of a hurry; why else leave the light on?

Samantha shook her head in an effort to jar all the conflicting thoughts free. Too many what-ifs and uncertainties that were pointless to consider. Her habit of dwelling on a possibility instead of acting on it needed to stop, she knew, or she'd find herself shaking again, eyes closed to the panic, hugging herself because there was nobody else to share her problems with. If only she had told Alice, confided in her big sis and spoken of her conflict, she would have the strength to fight her own battles.

Instead of standing in the open a moment longer, Samantha decided it was better to stay out of the light in case the man happened to return to the basement. She slipped into the shadows of the far corner, away from the hanging bulb that threw its light at the bottom of the steps.

A large, wooden table dominated this area of the basement. There wasn't enough light coming in at this angle to determine the color of the table's legs, and the top was covered—literally covered—with boxes of all sorts, large and small. Odds and ends spilled over from the topmost boxes in an avalanche of random assortments. No rhyme or reason to any of it. Just clutter. The kind people throw down below their main living quarters to forget about.

Discarded chairs, old rusted metal shelving, and neglected exercise equipment encircled the table, creating half a dozen nooks that Samantha could duck into if need be. Finer details emerged as her eyes adjusted to the shadowy corner, away from the brightness behind her.

Two items in the heap stood out to Samantha—the two halves of a wooden sign, split clean down the center, as if broken deliberately. When she joined them together, the red painted letters read HANSEN FAMILY FARMS.

The edges of the sign were smooth to the touch, the lettering still sharp and unfaded. This was a new sign, she realized. It wore imperfections from hanging outdoors, but it appeared to Samantha that the sign was taken down almost as recently as it had been put up.

She saw no post for the sign to hang upon, though her brief moment lying in the mud slick behind the Jeep's tire out front was spent looking away from the house, not at it, away from the man escorting her friends into his home at gunpoint. She hadn't seen or heard animals of any kind either, though they were likely taken to shelter due to the weather.

Samantha listened for sounds overhead, but all was drowned out by the relentless downpour of rain. She rubbed her hands up and down her arms in an attempt to generate some warmth. With the sun down, the air was getting cooler. The incessant leaking of water from the tiny windows didn't help the matter. It was cold water that froze her blood in her veins at the slightest touch. Thankfully, this corner of the floor remained dry.

Just then, everything on the shelves around her shook and threatened to fall. Samantha's heart raced as the whole of the house was rocked by what she hoped was only wind.

One moment later and all was still, and the sound of the rain continued.

This was probably not the safest place to be, Samantha realized. Another hit like that and any one of the shelves could come toppling down on her, pinning her against that cold floor, injured or dead. It was a more certain fate than Mr. Hansen stumbling upon her alive and well.

The only place she could think to hide for the moment was in that back room, the one Mr. Hansen and Julia had been in just minutes ago.

What could they have been doing in there for so long? Samantha knew her sense of time was hopelessly out of whack, but it must have been at least twenty minutes, maybe more. And when Julia emerged, she appeared unharmed to Samantha's eyes.

Curiosity got the better of her, and she found herself tiptoeing toward the back room. *Why are you tiptoeing? Nobody can hear you.* But it wasn't the sound that made her walk on the balls of her feet; when she stood flat-footed, the chill of the concrete shot a tingle up her back and neck that would not go away.

As she moved past the stairs and under the hanging bulb, Samantha spotted a collection of old footwear against the wall. A pair of women's sandals looked to be her size, and still in decent shape. It was a good idea, she thought, looking ahead to the cinderblock archway. From this vantage point, she saw a glow of light burning from the back room. There was a light source inside the room. Also now evident to Samantha was that the room had a dirt floor. This seemed odd, but bare footprints in the dirt would stand out, and neither Julia nor Mr. Hansen were barefoot.

Samantha eased down to a crouch, which was more difficult than she expected. Adrenaline had been pumping through her veins at breakneck speed when the shirt had landed on her head moments before, but now that her body had regulated itself back to a more normal state, the shooting pain in her side returned. She still didn't know the extent of the injury to her ribs, but she knew it was bad. She felt the weight of it, the sense of severity that remained no matter how hard she tried to push it away.

The sandals fit well enough, if a bit too big. She always hated her tiny feet. Made her look like a little girl, she thought. Nobody had ever commented on them, but Samantha was dissatisfied regardless. She didn't need the confirmation; *she* knew how she looked, which was not grown-up enough, with child-sized feet such as hers.

Nevertheless, it felt good to get her bare feet off the floor. A bit too big or not, there was a sense of security in feeling the old, leather straps wrapped around her feet, feeling the change of weight under each step. Samantha crept toward the back room powered by a tinge of confidence, ever so faint, but enough to set her body in motion.

The air was stale with a touch of sweetness, like how an underground gymnasium in an abandoned school might smell. Stepping into the archway, Samantha was met with a sight that stole every last ounce of confidence she thought she had seconds before.

A corpse, bloodied, face-down in the dirt beside a shallow grave.

Her hands went to her face, covering her eyes. A churning sensation rose from the pit of her stomach and up to the back of her throat quicker than human anatomy would allow. *Deep breaths, Samantha. Just take deep breaths. Calm yourself. It's all in your head.*

She swallowed. Her ribs throbbed. Heart pounded. She pulled her clammy hands from her face, looking away from the body. Only from her peripheral vision did she see the unknown figure's shoulder and arm, stiff from rigor mortis, pale from the lack of a heartbeat.

It's all in your head.

The sickening feeling was in her head—that much was true. But a dead person was on the ground less than ten feet from her. It wasn't anything she had experienced before in her twenty-two years of living.

Alice's funeral service was closed casket. It was the only funeral she had ever been to. All of her family was still alive, all of her friends and neighbors. She didn't get within twenty yards of Alice's casket. Didn't even want to look at it. Looking made it real. Being there in that room, in the closest thing to a family reunion she had ever known, made her understand that she wasn't dreaming. Samantha had never known life to be so cruel. Cruel and sudden. Driving to the river that one morning, no such thought could have ever entered her mind. It was an impossibility beyond her understanding.

On the drive home, with one less seat occupied in the family car, everything changed, yet it was all the same. Life went on for Samantha, just without her big sister by her side. Life went on for everyone but Alice. How Samantha was supposed to simply pick herself up and continue in the face of such a loss was a question that life provided no answer to. She cried herself to sleep for so many nights she stopped counting. Each night, she pondered that question, and each morning she awoke without an answer.

Maybe there was no answer, Samantha thought. Thinking about death is not living, she had decided, and agreed to Ted's insistence that she accompany him on this trip.

But death stood mere feet away from her now, a presence impossible to ignore.

Her first thought was not who the man was or how this came to be, but what was going to happen next. The second thought that invaded Samantha's mind was how long her friends upstairs had left before they joined this person about to be put into the earth. The gravity of the situation hit her with so much sudden force she had to sit down, sliding against the dusty wall to a crouch.

Her options were limited. There was little she could do

apart from bide her time until a window of opportunity opened. She could sneak up the stairs and slip the knife or the screwdriver to someone to use as a weapon, strike Mr. Hansen when he wasn't looking, maybe.

It sounded like it could work, Samantha mused. In theory. Executing the plan, on the other hand... She'd already missed a chance when Mr. Hansen was driving the Jeep behind the house. It's easy to be brave in your own mind, but far more difficult in the presence of danger; for Samantha, oftentimes impossible.

A crash startled her to her feet. Dirty fingers fumbled to open the box cutter. She held it in front of her like a shield, more of a threat than an actual defense. The sound resonated from directly above. It was a sound she recognized.

The slam of the screen door.

Footfalls beat against the wood of the back porch. The rain was too loud. Samantha scrambled to the nearest tiny window and strained on her tiptoes to look out.

Her view of the back yard was poor, but she saw enough to know the sounds were not coming from her untrustworthy imagination. Mr. Hansen stepped through enormous puddles in his stride toward the parked Jeep.

Samantha's head turned on a swivel, falling on the steps leading up to the first floor.

THIRTEEN

GETTING OUT WAS EASIER SAID than done. Bobby had been wrestling against his bindings every chance he got, but to no avail. His wrists felt moist, whether from sweat or blood or both.

But now he sat still, his concern shifted toward Julia, who sat across the room with her head back and her eyes closed. He saw the pain written on her face, in the beads of perspiration that slid down the strands of her black hair in little droplets.

Whatever Michael had done to her down in the cellar, he was going to pay for it, Bobby promised himself. He wasn't going to wait to find out what it was, either. He was going to strike first and let whoever found Michael's broken body later ask the questions. He just had to get free from these god damn ties.

Ted had said it was a bad idea, but Ted never thought realistically. He was too analytical. Write his thoughts on paper and it all sounds great, but the real world isn't written on paper. Variables change, opponents alter their strategy unexpectedly; you have to roll with the punches while throwing a few of your own. Bobby knew how big of a risk it was to mount an offensive against this man, but it was a risk they had to take.

The first priority now was Julia. Safety second. Michael would return from outside in a moment with her painkillers, which would help, but she needed a comfortable resting place, at the very least. If she was hurt beyond that, a hospital visit was in order.

Two months from now, they would be married. The thought still seemed like a fantasy to Bobby. His mind was never on marriage. Growing up, he wanted no part of it. Thought it was a terrible idea, an antiquated ceremony that had no place or function in modern society. *Most marriages fail; why would I want to be a part of that?* he would ask himself. He never once pondered the answer. As good as things always seemed to be between him and Julia, his mind was made up. Julia never brought it up, either. They were just happy to be together.

But something had changed in Bobby, sitting in the hospital next to Julia's bed after her accident. She went nearly fifty hours without saying one word to anyone after learning that her days on the ski slopes were all behind her and that her Olympic dreams would never come true. It was the most time Bobby had spent alone in his own head. What he learned that day was that he didn't have any dreams that meant more to him than Julia. Them being happy together was the one thing he wanted above all else. Having that reality nearly snatched from his grasp in his girlfriend's near-fatal skiing accident made everything suddenly clear.

Julia was put through a rigorous rehabilitation to get back on her feet—literally. The damage to her spine, coupled with the previous several weeks of being bedridden had done something to her legs; they didn't want to work quite as well as they once did. She had explained that it felt akin to learning a new skill—frustrating and difficult to start, but Julia was a fast learner, and her near-superhuman powers of determination and self-confidence had her up and about before any doctor, nurse, or rehab therapist could have dreamed.

Her first steps after suffering the catastrophic fall came with the assistance of a physical therapist and guided handrails, but the driving force was Bobby at the opposite end, urging her forward, shouting words of encouragement and she shuffled toward him one step at a time.

When Julia was but feet away from Bobby—two or three steps at the most—he bent one knee and showed her the ring. The look on her face said it all. He didn't even have to ask, and she never had the chance to answer. They knew.

It was the only time Bobby had seen Julia cry.

But now she wore a different look, one which spoke of a desire to leave this place, to find a comfortable bed somewhere, lie down next to her fiancé, and close her eyes until the pain went away.

"Hang in there, babe," Bobby said. He wanted to do more, so much more, but this was all that was within his power.

"It's not bad," Julia replied, moving only her mouth, her eyes remaining shut.

Bobby knew it was a lie. If Julia was on her deathbed, she would be saying the same thing. The girl knew no defeat. Her strength was endless.

A sound from the kitchen drew the attention of the room. It was the creak of the basement door swinging idly on its hinges, and a soft knock of the brass knob against the wallpaper followed.

Ted stole a second to glance to the back door—no sign of Michael. He hadn't yet returned.

Carla, with no view of the kitchen or basement door at all, jumped her gaze from Ted to Bobby and back again. "What's going on?" Her voice was just below a meek whisper, barely recognizable as words.

Bobby heard a pressure put upon the ancient floorboards just out of view. Approaching covertly, not wanting to be heard. One shy step, then another.

Then another.

Until the near-unrecognizable figure of a young woman stood silhouetted by the strobe lighting images playing across the TV screen.

Another step and the figure that emerged from the shadows was a far cry from the girl who had rode shotgun in the Jeep on the trip to this far-flung farmhouse. Mud dried in a crust that covered her left side, knee to shoulder. The tight, bouncy curls of her hair fell in beleaguered tangles. She wore a soggy tank-top and denim shorts, each the color of dirt, with only the faintest trace of their true yellow and blue. A trickle of dried blood curved down the side of her forehead toward her ear, and she kept one arm close to her lower ribcage.

In her other hand there was a familiar object—the box-cutter used to cut the ties on Julia's wrists. The tool was unfolded, prepared for use.

Ted was too shocked to speak, though his face lit up when his eyes met with Samantha's. The key to freedom was within ten feet.

A car door shut.

Samantha's eyes broke away from Ted and snapped to

the back door. Footsteps approached. Michael was on his way back in. No time to cut anyone free; she would be seen and Michael had not slipped up in leaving without his shotgun behind. It stuck to his hands as if a part of him, an extension of his very being.

Samantha dropped to a crouch, supporting her ribs. The extent of her injuries was unknown.

A torrent of rainfall announced Michael opening the back door.

If Samantha didn't act now, she would be as good as dead, as with everyone else tied up in this home. Mouthing the words "I'm sorry," she placed the box-cutter on the hardwood floor, aimed for Ted, and gave it a push.

The sound it made, metal dragging against weathered wood, seemed impossibly loud. No doubt Michael had heard, even over the storm.

At once, the box-cutter stopped sliding. It came to rest inches from Ted's feet. Fate had conspired to bring them to this point, and now it was conspiring to make sure they never again saw the light of day.

All hope died in Samantha's eyes. It was a look of absolute failure. She had a chance, took the shot, and blew it. Her mouth hung agape at the loss of what was likely to be her only chance at extending her friends a helping hand. She just hadn't extended far enough. Samantha backpedaled, melting into the shadows, fading away as if life itself had just abandoned her.

Ted extended his legs as far as he could. The heel of his shoe was barely able to touch the box-cutter. And Michael was now in the house.

In a moment of sheer determination, live-or-die instincts took over and Ted swung his right leg at the box-cutter. He connected with a back heel-kick, which sent the tool sliding under the radiator to which he and Bobby were tied.

Out of sight.

Michael stepped into the room carrying Julia's pain-killers. He was the only one not holding his breath. Bobby's glare locked on Julia as Michael fed her one of the pills from the bottle, then another and then a third.

Bobby felt the box-cutter bump against his knuckles after Ted kicked it out of view—an action that had probably just saved everyone's lives. Michael would have had some questions about how the tool found itself in the middle of the living room floor, opened, with all guests tied up securely by their host.

Ted breathed a sigh of relief when those questions were not asked. But Bobby was unable to relax just yet. He had to see this man walk away from Julia. He had to find that box-cutter. It was back there, behind him under the radiator somewhere, inches away at most.

His fingers brushed metal. It was an effort to stretch for the object without drawing attention to himself. His stone cold glare was enough of a beacon. A man on edge such as Michael would not benefit from any confrontation, physical or mental, and it would not help Bobby's situation either. But he had to hold that box-cutter in his hands.

If only his fingers were a tad longer. He felt the warmth of the handle against his fingertips. Samantha must have been holding on to it for dear life. How in the hell did she even come to find it in her possession? Hiding the entire time without Michael knowing, stealing away his weapons from right under his nose; that was no small feat for anyone, let alone someone as timid and naturally passive as Sam.

Bobby needed that box-cutter. Needed to hold it in his fingers, cut himself free, and do something—some offensive action—before Michael knew it was missing. Julia was in no shape to assist in any more chores, and he didn't seem to be a cruel man; just a man in an unfortunate situation. Just like Bobby. He too was a man in an unfortunate situation. And as Michael took action to escape from his circumstances, someone would have to do the same for Julia and Ted and Samantha, as well.

The thought of Michael asking for more aid swirled about in Bobby's head, clouding all other judgment. He'll need the cutter to free either of his two hostages from the radiator, or that Carla lady from the adjacent room.

Doubtful, though, that she would be freed to be put to work.

No, the only way Carla would be free of those bindings, Bobby knew, would be to accompany the man from the kitchen, her lover, down the basement steps to be put to rest eternally. Bobby had already made up his mind. He would make sure the same fate did not befall Julia, himself, Ted, or Samantha. Whatever needed to be done to assure that their future existed in Rockaway Beach, Oregon, would be done.

With the tips of two fingers, Bobby held the box-cutter against the floor and ever so delicately pulled it toward him. The first half dozen attempts ended in abrupt failure. He just had to hold it at the right angle, on the right floorboard, pull at the right speed with the right amount of pressure, all in the right amount of time.

All the while, Bobby's eyes tracked the movements of the man with the shotgun. When Michael was finished with the business of Julia and her painkillers, he capped the bottle, set it on the coffee table alongside the trio of cell phones, and collapsed into his spot on the couch once again. His eyelids fell shut and the only company was the sound of the wind and rain battering the home's exterior with a force that equaled the burning desire within Bobby to grab that god damn box-cutter and end this day before long.

Within moments, he had worked the box-cutter into the grasp of his fingers. Now came the more difficult part—maneuvering it so the blade rested against his restraints and not his flesh. Doing so without dropping the object with a loud *klunk* against the foot of the radiator or a thud against the floor, working blind with limited motion, was the real challenge.

Michael seemed in no haste to continue whatever project he had Julia toiling with in the basement, completed or not.

Julia, too, sat with her head back, eyes shut, not saying a word. She appeared to be more at peace as the pills took effect. Drowsiness is what the label said, but oftentimes they knocked her out for at least half an hour at the dosage Michael had just administered.

That could work against his plan, Bobby considered. Julia needing help would no doubt hinder their escape, and Bobby wanted to be out the door, in the Jeep, and back on the highway in one swift, smooth stroke. Ten seconds, max. That's all he would allow. Once he K.O.ed Michael, they would be gone, and all this would be only a memory.

As Bobby worked the blade against the cable ties that held his wrists in place, he felt Ted's eyes glued to his every move. Nobody said a word.

Another set of eyes hovered over Bobby as he worked

ever so delicately. He felt the whole room watching.

Waiting.

Knowing.

Without warning, Michael stood. He locked an absent glare on Carla and stepped toward her. There was something odd about his movements… Whereas before he was jittery, on edge, now he stood tall, confident in his actions. It was a subtle change, but Bobby picked up on it, trained to study the subtleties of his opponents on the mat from his wrestling days.

As Michael neared Carla, a grin spread across his unshaven, unwashed face, turning up the corners of his mouth in a twisted deformation that could almost be mistaken for a smile. "I spent a lot of time thinking, babe," Michael said to her, "thinking about how to move past this, back to a life of normalcy. But you know what?" He let the question hang.

Carla raised terrified eyes to meet him, tear-streaks rushing over her round cheeks. "I… I don't know, Michael."

"I couldn't think of a way."

"Michael, wait a minute, please," Carla pleaded through sobs. "There's always a way, Michael. Baby, please, there's always a way. It's all up to us, don't you see? It doesn't have to be this way."

"You know, you've been making some pretty poor decisions lately. Inviting that man into our home—*my* home." Michael turned away; his 'smile' vanished.

Carla sniffled, and spoke in a voice softer than before. "Don't trap yourself in a corner, Michael. We can wipe the slate clean and start over. Don't you want that, Michael? Baby? Don't you want that?"

"No," Michael answered, his back to Carla.

Then he turned, raised the shotgun—and pulled the trigger.

FOURTEEN

FOR A SECOND, THE storm vanished. There was no further sound of rainfall, no more wind beating against the siding, no more words spoken. All sound in the house was silenced—except for the blast of the shotgun and the subsequent ringing in Ted's ears.

That one second passed, and what followed was the shattering of glass, the rending of wood, and the breaking of the small metal hinges that held the doors to the china cabinet in place. The shot had ripped through Carla's flesh with surreal ease, splintering bone and perforating vital organs. Her dead weight dropped instantly, and with her came the china cabinet doors to which her wrists were still tied, collapsing to the floor in a cacophony of glass and debris, and the solid thump of another victim.

A crimson wake crept out from below the body. Michael stared straight ahead, shotgun still held in the firing position, smoking. There was nothing in his stare that hinted at emotion. He was a vacant shell of a man, now, his eyes fixed absently ahead on the crystal wine glasses and priceless family heirlooms that tumbled to the floor in pieces, blasted into fragments with the simple pull of a trigger.

Never to be repaired.

The first afforded glance of Carla's left hand confirmed Ted's suspicions—a wedding ring. He felt the gravity of the situation sit heavy on his chest. None of this could be repaired, he thought. Michael knew that. His relationship—his marriage to this woman—was over hours ago. It had concluded before he had opened the door to find Julia and Bobby standing on his front porch.

Now, it was official.

The ringing in Ted's ears persisted, but his thoughts were with Samantha. She was alive, but hurt. The fall she took rounding the Jeep had been worse than he thought. If she had broken ribs, they would need to get out of there sooner rather than later. Time was not their ally.

Before Samantha had appeared with the box-cutter, Ted had been convinced it was a bad idea to fight back, to mount an escape, to do anything that would make them Michael's enemies.

Everything had changed.

It was good that Bobby had found the box-cutter under the radiator. It meant they had a chance of fighting back, and Bobby had never lost a fight in his life. Not that Ted knew, anyway. But while Bobby was surely stronger than Ted, he lacked patience. Ted didn't know what Bobby's plan was, but knowing Bobby, it probably didn't involve waiting longer than they needed to. However, Ted was positive it didn't involve rushing an unstable man who had just murdered his wife in cold blood, either.

Wheels were already spinning in Ted's head, formulating a plan. It had appeared that Samantha came up from the basement, though he had no clear, direct view of the doorway leading down the stairs. He did have line of sight on the front door and the steps leading to the second floor, and she had not come from either of those directions. It was also unlikely that she used the back door, which Michael had just used himself.

If she was still down in the basement, that must mean there was another way in, another door that had access to the outside. *Of course; it's a god damn house.* And if Samantha could get inside, they could get outside.

Ted chewed this over. It felt like a sound plan. The Jeep had been moved to the back yard, so going out the front would be a waste of precious seconds. The back door would make the most sense. Julia didn't look herself. She wouldn't handle the basement steps well. Her eyelids fluttered on the edge of consciousness. The boom of the shotgun had jarred her momentarily, but whatever drugs she was on, they were strong. On top of an empty stomach, no less.

But the wheels in Ted's mind came to an abrupt halt at the first sound of Michael's voice, speaking to his deceased wife. "Well, look at that, Carla. The slate has been cleaned. Guess we can start over now." There was blood pooling against the soles of his boots, seeping between the treads.

Ted wanted to say something about what had just happened. He always seemed to have the right words that a friend or family member needed to hear to help put things at ease. But now, for the first time in as far back as memory would allow, nothing came to mind. Not a single word.

There was nothing to say. Resigned to this fact, Ted sat with his mouth closed. Helpless. These were events far beyond his control. This woman and her mystery lover had an arrangement long before Ted piloted the Jeep down the long dirt path to this house's front porch. Now this woman was lying dead on the floor in a pile of debris; the lover down in the basement, likely rotting in a damp corner. This was going to happen whether Ted was there or not, he realized. That could not be stopped.

"You didn't want to sell the farm, and look where that had landed us," Michael continued. "You didn't want to move to the city, and look where that got us. Staying here in this dying place! Well, you get to stay, after all."

He stormed across the room in no particular direction. Just large, heavy, indeterminate steps leaving bloody boot prints behind. There was something in his eyes, Ted noticed, but he couldn't pinpoint what it was. They were the same dark, sullen eyes as before, but now they were awake.

A bump against Ted's foot came from Bobby's direction. They met eyes, and Bobby's furtive glance fell to where his hands were tied.

Had been tied.

The thick cable tie that secured his wrists to the other end of the radiator now sat on the floor behind him, out of view, sprinkled with drops of a dark liquid. In his right hand, Bobby held the box-cutter. The dim light cast a crimson hue on the wet blade.

Bobby had freed himself through considerable effort. His wrists bled from minor cuts. He remained seated, pretending he was still tied up.

"You." The declaration cast in Ted's direction nearly made him jump out of his skin. His eyes snapped in Michael's direction and met with the end of the shotgun barrel.

Had Michael seen what Ted saw? Ted was unsure;

though absolutely sure his heart had stopped beating for at least two seconds.

"Yes, you," Michael said to Ted and nobody else. "You're going to help me this time."

Stunned, Ted fumbled for words. All he could muster was a stumbling, "M-me?"

"The girl was too weak. She can't help me anymore."

"I'll do it," Bobby chimed in. His words did not reach Michael, who held all of this attention on Ted.

"Look," said Ted, "We can help you. We *want* to help you. I think we can help each other figure this all out."

Michael stood upright, baffled. "Figure what out? There's nothing to figure out. What's done is done."

"I know, but … nothing else needs to be … done."

A pause from Michael as the statement registered. "Kid, I know what you're saying, but this is what needs to happen: you need to help me carry that body down into the basement and clean up this mess."

Bobby raised his voice, making sure he was heard. "Why don't I help you instead?"

This time, Michael turned to Bobby. "Why? Does your friend here have a bad back, too?"

Ted almost had himself convinced that Bobby was going to leap up and slash Michael's throat with the box-cutter that instant but, remarkably, Bobby maintained his cool. There was a fury inside, no question about it, but Bobby had decided not to act on it just yet. Maybe it was the shotgun that Michael still held in his right hand. One shot had already been used; doubtful he was afraid to use the second.

Michael swung the aim of the shotgun between Ted and Bobby. "Another thing that needs to happen is that you two remember who makes the decisions around here. I don't have the time or patience for questions."

"We just don't want anyone else to get hurt," Ted said with tones of surrender. He wanted tones of compromise, but fear kept it from coming out that way.

A sudden fit of rage exploded within Michael, like a bomb that had been counting down and just now hit zero. "I don't want anyone to get hurt, either! What do you think; I'm some kind of animal? I just go around throwing everyone down the cellar if they don't agree with me?"

"No, of course you—"

Michael pointed the shotgun at Carla's corpse. "None of this would have happened if it wasn't for her and that guy she was with. I don't even know who he was! But I have to pay the price for what they did. Is that fair?"

The severity of their situation had become starkly clear to Ted. Michael was not the calm and quiet individual he had appeared to be in the early stages of their imprisonment. This was a man who had lost control, and was doing everything he could think of to regain command of his life, going to extreme lengths to, as he put it, wipe the slate clean.

Even Michael's choice of words were telling; having to 'pay the price' for what his wife had done, as if there was no way of escaping her actions or their impact on his life.

"No, it's not fair," Michael said in answer to his own question, as if there was no other answer. As if the answer was completely obvious.

Ted swallowed hard before asking the question he didn't want to ask. "What would you have us do?"

Michael stared at Ted, moments of silence building between the two of them.

It occurred to Ted then that Michael still had zero ideas of what to do with his captives. This both calmed and terrified Ted in equal amounts. Calm because he still did not yet think to simply blast away with the shotgun and bury their bodies somewhere on his property; terrified because a man in Michael's mental state should not be making life or death decisions. One had been made minutes earlier, the end result being another body on the floor and more blood to wipe away.

"You're going to help me clean this up before anything else happens," Michael said. "Then we can talk about your release."

Release. It was not a word Michael had used before in their time there. Visions of having his hands and those of his friends unbound danced through Ted's mind like a temptation.

Was it possible Michael would let them go? Maybe he was resigned to his fate after murdering his wife, giving up on facing the reality that his life could not go on as planned. A new path was being carved out for him—*by* him. Where this path was leading, nobody knew. Not even Michael. But Ted's path seemed sunlit and clear of rubble.

Release.

Whether or not Bobby had heard the word in the same way that Ted had did not register on Bobby's face. He sat still as a statue, stiller than before. Watching and waiting. Hearing, but not listening.

This was a bad time, Ted thought. A very bad time for Bobby to be free to his own devices. He, too, was a man under great emotional distress. Life or death decisions should not be in his hands, nor should the box-cutter.

The options were before them—play along and hope

for an act of compassion from this unstrung captor, or fight back. A lesser of two evils, Ted knew.

Naturally, he found little fault in option number one, but he knew that his view was not shared by Bobby. Sooner or later, they might have to resort to option number two, but until they knew for sure if they would have to…

"Bobby, it's cool. I'll help him out." Ted turned to Michael. "If you get some scissors, I'll be able to clean this all up."

Scissors. Not a box-cutter. Not a knife. Take his mind away from that. Make him think of a totally different object, one that operates in a different manner yet would still get the job of severing the ties done. Ted thought his plan might work. He felt a hint of confidence about it. His words came out easier this time, but a knot of fear still sat at the core of his abdomen, tightening, not going anywhere.

Michael's free hand went to the front pocket of his jeans but came out empty. He swapped the shotgun to his free hand and checked the other pocket. This was also empty.

The box-cutter.

He was looking for it. Ted felt his eyes getting heavy, falling in the direction of Bobby's fists, held behind his back in a charade of captivity, gripping the opened box-cutter in white knuckles.

No, don't look. Do not look. He doesn't know. He can't know. It's impossible. Samantha brought it up from the basement; Michael would check down there before interrogating Bobby.

Michael displayed no outward signs of curiosity as to where the box-cutter disappeared to. In fact, he treated its whereabouts as insignificant to the moment.

Without a word or so much as a glance to tell his audience he was about to leave the room, Michael was gone. They, too, were insignificant to Michael. His world existed inside his own head. All that was and will be, everything of consequence, resided in the torment of his own thoughts.

It was a frightening concept to entertain, but not half as terrifying as the idea of Michael returning to the basement, to the exact spot where he left the box-cutter, only to stumble upon Samantha's hiding place.

Samantha. Where did she go? Was she safe again? Was she even safe before? A hundred-thousand questions inundated Ted's thoughts at once, emotion overwhelming rational thought. But one notion took center stage in front of all others—the prospect of never having another opportunity to tell Samantha how he felt about her.

Growing up, it was never a secret that Ted had a thing for Samantha's sister. They were still children at the time, only then starting to see the opposite sex in a different light as they began to grow into young adulthood. Ted started to look at Alice as more than just a friend he rode bikes with.

He thought at the time that their newfound 'relation-ship' would last forever, as all children assumed. And adults, too, Ted considered. Michael probably thought the same about Carla. Once married, they would move in together, start a family, and eventually grow old together, rocking side by side on the front porch swing every evening after supper.

Nothing lasts forever. As sure as Ted knew that to be true, the fact did little to ease the pain of a rejected heart. He rode his bike alone after Alice had met a new 'friend'. Long nights he spent on that bike, searching for those same feelings elsewhere—the good feelings when people are together and every minute of the day is filled with joy and life has you convinced, just for a moment, that maybe this *will* last forever. No force could possibly sever a bond so pure.

Ted didn't realize it at the time, but he spent most of those nights alone not thinking of Alice, but of Samantha. Where Alice was honest in everything she said and did, Samantha was an enigma. You had to dig very deep to have an idea of who she really was. Ted wasn't sure he had ever known—even at this moment, waiting to be cut free from the radiator for the first time since their arrival.

Samantha was free. Bobby freed himself. Julia had been freed. Ted was the only one of them who hadn't tasted that freedom. He didn't know why, but a feeling of sadness crept over him, subtle, like a deepening shadow. It was strange, he thought. He was always the one with the ideas, the plans, the desire to lead. Where was that leadership now? It had gotten him nowhere. He hadn't moved since he first sat down in front of that radiator, and their situation had not gotten much better.

Catching that fleeting glimpse of Samantha as she emerged from seemingly out of nowhere caused that knot of fear to pull tighter. Her current state brought Ted no comfort; she was hurt and needed help. But the mere act of seeing her, knowing she was so close but still out of reach, only made Ted more aware of how tight the cables ties were around his wrists.

His arms were immobile. Blood swelled in his fingers. He could wiggle them, but barely. It was past time that he was cut free.

There was a sound of rummaging through kitchen

drawers as Michael searched for scissors. The next thing Ted knew, he was sitting alone at the radiator.

Bobby was on his feet, moving toward the wall that divided the living room and kitchen. He was quick and silent as a shadow, surprisingly nimble for his stature. He crouched beyond the archway, out of Michael's view.

Box-cutter in hand.

Ready to pounce.

FIFTEEN

THE COMMOTION OVERHEAD EXPLODED LIKE thunder.

Samantha knelt in a dark corner of the basement, hands clasped tight over her ears. She didn't want to hear what was happening, couldn't bear to hear the damage she had just caused. A madness of footsteps stomped out of rhythm, heavy against opposition, grunting, swearing, slamming into walls. She heard every shout, every scream, everything.

A thudding of bodies hit the floor. What sounded like a heavy metallic object skidded across the wood above. Could be the shotgun. Could be something else. In a life or death struggle, anything could be a weapon.

Tears were falling down Samantha's cheeks before she had even made it to the bottom of the basement steps. *What have I done?* Everything was wrong. Everything. She made the wrong choice. Instead of helping her friends, she put them in more danger.

Whatever was happening upstairs was her fault.

Stupid, stupid, STUPID!

She had thought it to be the right choice, that she would be helpful, but she found her judgment to be dead wrong.

More slams from above. The shouting did not stop. Julia was screaming Bobby's name. Curses flew from every mouth with a venom Samantha had never before heard in her life. Heads pounding the floor, boots scrambling, bodies toppling again over furniture upon standing; it was a chaos of sounds, an attack on her senses. Samantha squeezed her eyes shut as tight as they would close, but the horror that played on in her mind could not be silenced.

Then a shot rang out.

Deafening. Samantha screamed. She wanted to keep screaming, scream until she ran out of voice and all breath had escaped her. Scream until she passed out. Scream until she awoke in her own bed, realizing this whole day was nothing but a nightmare.

But it wasn't a nightmare. She had already tried to end it on her own, and the end result was a conflict that would likely result in another death—the death of the homeowner, Mr. Hansen, the man who had his life ripped out from under him earlier in the day, or the death of one of her friends. She didn't even know who was fighting. Who got free? The knife hadn't reached Ted or Bobby. She'd even failed in that.

A death on her conscience was a weight Samantha thought she would never have to bear.

Her head began to ache from pressing her hands to her ears so hard. The shotgun blast was unmistakable. It was the same gut-wrenching sound she had heard earlier. She wanted to puke. She wanted to scream. There were a thousand things she wanted to do, but there was nothing more she could manage.

The one chance she had was blown. That's why Samantha never took chances. She wasn't any good at them.

Either the fault was with her, or fate simply enjoyed being unkind to her. It wasn't a feeling one could get used to. The pain of this moment was a sharp as any other, driving into her heart a blade that never dulled, inflicting wounds that never healed.

She wanted to kick herself for such a weak attempt, but her body was frozen, kneeling on the hard concrete of the basement floor, shaking hands clasped over her ears, head down and eyes shut to the world.

Adrenaline shot through her veins. Her heart raced. She had to make a conscious effort to breathe, and breathe deep. The throbbing pain in her ribs was gone; that only frightened her more. It was going to come back hard when her body caught up to her emotions. Samantha needed to calm herself. At that moment, it was the one thing she knew for certain.

Their drive that morning felt like a lifetime ago, a dream rather than a memory. Time was at a standstill ever since the Jeep left the main highway to search for shelter. Darkness came over the skies and had turned day into night, minutes into hours, and hours into what felt like days. With it came the storm, and the rain still fell.

A shiver rocked Samantha's shoulders. It reminded her, strangely, of the previous day's drive—a blazing August day, heat without humidity, and a sun unmasked by any cloud cover. The air conditioning had given up, and rolling the windows down did little to combat the oppressive heat trapped inside the vehicle. Samantha had to squint behind her sunglasses, the day was so bright. Five minutes into the drive and she was already gross with sweat.

At the time, she thought she should have stayed in the shower that morning, cold water pouring down on her head, the crappy motel plumbing affording little warmth. There had been no functioning air conditioning in any of the rooms, so the coldness of the water was welcomed. It was a shock at first and it took a moment before Samantha became acclimated to the temperature, but once that moment passed, her body and mind all at once felt refreshed.

Ted did not have the same experience. He was in and out of the shower quicker than Samantha thought possible, and ready to stop for breakfast before hitting the road. He said nothing of the night before.

Bobby shared a room with Julia, his reasoning being in case she needed anything during the night. She was still recovering from her accident and sleeping was often an uncomfortable experience for her. It involved a lot of time spent lying awake, restless, turning away from an uncomfortable position in search of elusive sleep.

This, of course, meant that Samantha and Ted would have to share a room—and a bed—a situation they had never found themselves in before. At first Samantha wanted to protest, but something inside told her to remain quiet. It would be an experience, and the reason she agreed to come along was to step outside of her comfort zone. She wanted to make a conscious effort to grow as a person, and knew that this would often, if not always, challenge her.

It seemed to Samantha that Ted had fallen asleep as soon as his head hit the pillow that night. He was never one for wasting time. It was only natural that he and Alice were drawn to one another. They both had a proclivity for experiencing the most of what life had to offer, albeit in different fashions. It was only natural, then, that their relationship would end not long after it had officially begun.

As far back as she could remember, a horde of random thoughts swam in Samantha's mind each night with nothing she could do to quell their tide. She lived life internally. Lying next to Ted, her mind found a peculiar stillness. No longer were her thoughts concerned with what *might* happen, but what had the possibility of happening at this moment.

It was a sobering thought that kept her up hours into the night. She had spent countless hours—days, even—pondering possibilities that seemed unlikely after a rational reexamination. Wasted time, she thought. Hours she would never get back.

It was a choice she made that had gotten her to where she was, lying next to Ted in the stillness of the night, feeling only the rising and falling of his chest as he breathed those drawn-out breaths of deep sleep. In that moment, she wanted to reach her hand out and place it on his chest, wrap it around him and pull herself closer, until their bodies were flush against one another, and stay that way until morning.

The puppet-strings of impulse had lifted her hand and brought it upon Ted, but a touch of fear made her recoil at the last instant. Instead of his chest, she settled for his shoulder. It was only a minute before Ted had taken Samantha by the hand and rolled onto his side, putting her hand where she had wanted it, easing her body closer to his. She glided her head over to the edge of his pillow and closed her eyes.

Samantha fell into a deeper sleep than she had ever known.

She awoke in the morning to the warmth of dawn

shining through the window into her eyes. When in the night she had turned the opposite direction, Samantha did not know, but now, curled up to nobody but herself, she was awake, and Ted still slumbered.

Their late-night interaction was not spoken of by either of them. It was doubtful to her that Ted even remembered doing it. He did not act as if he had any recollection of it.

Julia and Bobby took a nap in the back seat of the Jeep later that morning after stopping for breakfast. Ted pulled in the best radio station he could find. Classic rock; it was something they could all agree on. Who didn't enjoy CCR? They jammed out a Marvin Gaye cover for what felt like half an hour while the vehicle's occupants sat (or slept) in silence.

Samantha tried to think of a way to broach the subject with Ted about last night, but every idea she formulated was met with an equally strong counter argument. She never thought of herself as a very talented person, but one thing she could do better than anyone was talk herself out of an uncomfortable situation.

But on this day, she was determined not to let that happen. She wanted to look fear in the eyes and realize the person looking back was only herself. But how to bring it up? What to say? What if he didn't remember, or didn't find it as comforting as she did? That would make a long ride even longer, sitting in the heat and the awkwardness, wishing she could take her words back.

Samantha never had the chance to decide what to say. They were driving headlong into the storm. The winds had nearly shoved the Jeep clear off the highway. It was then Ted made the decision to take the next exit and find somewhere to wait it out. An encounter with the first tornado Samantha had ever seen had Ted slamming on the brakes, flooring the vehicle in reverse, and speeding to the first building they saw.

This home.

It was hot the previous day, but now Samantha was cold. Only now did she realize she was kneeling in a puddle. The rainfall showed no signs of stopping. It hammered against the house, unrelenting. Water spilled in through the cracks around the tiny basement windows at a heavier rate than before.

Samantha rose to her feet, and the pain in her side increased with her every movement. She couldn't stop shivering. Now it wasn't even clear to her if she was cold or not. Her body might be reacting to her injury. She was sweating and shivering.

The fighting upstairs had ceased.

There was no sound coming from above. Samantha strained to hear, but the wind pounding the rainfall against every window of the house was preposterously loud. Never before did she hear a noise this loud in nature. She couldn't even hear herself breathe.

No footsteps. Why are there no footsteps?

A terror grew in Samantha's chest. Something had happened upstairs. Something *bad*.

The struggle was over, and she felt with the utmost certainty that one of her friends was dead. Ted, Bobby, Julia … all three of them, perhaps. But it was too quiet for it to have been Mr. Hansen. No, there would surely still be movement, a mad scramble to free one another and rush down the basement steps to take Samantha by the hand and lead her out of this home and this nightmare forever.

Samantha shuffled toward the center of the basement.

115

Maybe a different vantage point could afford a better opportunity to hear what was happening.

But nothing was happening.

Then she saw it, from the corner of her eye…

Light, playing in the droplets that clung to the exterior of one of those tiny basement windows. Red light, flashing on and off again.

Samantha moved to the window; the pain in her side was an afterthought now.

As she got closer, another light appeared. This one blue.

She could not see out of the window, but the lights continued to flash. On and off again. Red then blue. Red then blue again.

The realization hit Samantha in the chest with enough force to knock the wind clear from her lungs and stir a flutter in her heart.

Her call for help worked. It *actually* worked.

The police had finally arrived.

SIXTEEN

"DON'T MOVE. DON'T say one god damn word."

Michael held the box-cutter in Bobby's direction, a thick drop of blood hanging from the end of its dull blade. He backed away from where Bobby knelt on the floor, easing toward where his dead wife's body lay.

With one quick movement, he grabbed the china cabinet by its top with his free hand and pulled the whole thing down in a sudden rush of sound and fury. Whoever was outside may have heard the thunderous collapse, but it now covered the corpse and the blood that had seeped from it, effectively masking the scene from any spectator's prying eyes.

Ted held his breath as Michael approached. He reached behind and cut the bindings from Ted's swollen wrists then wasted no time shoving him toward an armchair that sat in the corner of the living room.

"Get over there and sit. No words," Michael commanded. He turned on Bobby. "You—in that other chair. Do it now."

Bobby wiped a knuckle against his lip and it came away red. From his hands and knees, he lifted heated eyes to Michael.

It was only when Michael moved for Julia that Bobby lifted himself up and slowly did as he was instructed. Michael grabbed a fist of Julia's hair, pulled her head back, and rested the blade against the flesh of her neck. "Here's what's going to happen…"

Red and blue lights swirled through the downpour beyond the curtained windows. A car door slammed shut.

"…You do as I say, and you say *nothing* about this. One wrong word and she dies…"

Footsteps marched up the wooden steps of the front porch.

"…Don't try to be a hero…"

A knock against the front door.

"…Because you will lose."

"State police."

Michael cut the ties from Julia's hands and kicked them behind the TV, out of sight. Julia could hardly stand by herself. She leaned on Michael for support as he led her to the couch. "Lie down and don't move," he said then picked up the shotgun and dropped it behind the same couch where it, too, would be out of sight.

Another rap of knuckles on the other side of the door. "Anybody home? Mike, you in there?"

Ted turned a glance to Bobby, who sat in his designated chair unmoving. His eyes stuck to Michael like glue, refusing to accept what had just happened.

He had lost the fight.

Ted thought about saying something to Bobby, maybe something about not saying a word and doing what he was told and all that, but it would only be wasted breath. Julia was on the couch at the opposite end of the room, and Michael had the weapon. He had the upper hand. There was nothing Bobby could do to remedy this situation. Nothing except sit still and shut up. Any outburst and Julia would suffer more than she already had.

Michael strode to the front door, composed himself as best he could in that second before his hand hit the knob, and then the door opened to invite the cataclysmic wrath of howling winds and storm-tossed rains.

It was so loud they had to shout to be heard five feet from one another. Michael turned aside and welcomed the state trooper into his home.

Ted judged him to be on the down-slope of his fifties, toes already dipped in the waters of retirement. He wore a state-issued poncho and a covered hat to keep the rainfall at bay, though it appeared to be useless in this weather.

The state trooper shook himself off. "Thanks, Mike. It's coming down like a mother out there."

"No problem. Come inside and have a seat." Michael offered an old, wooden rocking chair. The trooper crossed the floor and sat, nodding politely at the two gentlemen seated in the far corner and the young lady upon the couch.

"Been in and out of that damn car all night. Town sees a little bit of rain and everyone goes nuts."

Michael rested on the arm of the couch, close to Julia. "Don't I know it."

"If I'd known you had guests, I would have—"

Michael waved it off. "It's fine. Just some kids passing through. That's Ted and Bobby, this is Julia."

The trooper tipped his hat to them with a smile, raindrops spilling from the brim. "Looking for some shelter during this weather. Always a smart idea." The trooper looked over the disheveled nature of the room. "Though it doesn't look to be much safer indoors, either."

"The winds are unbelievable," Michael said. "We think it was a twister that came a little too close to the house. Knocked everything all over the place." He showed his forearm to the state trooper and the 5-inch slash near his elbow. "This is what I get for trying to save it."

Michael's eyes chanced a look across the room where they met Bobby's hardened stare.

The state trooper removed his poncho. "Consider yourself lucky, Mike. Could have been a lot worse. What about that girl there… Julia is your name?"

She nodded a weak nod.

"She'll be fine," Michael said. "Wasn't feeling well earlier. Said she just needs to rest a while." He cleared his throat and changed the subject. "So, Lou, what brings you out this way in this kind of weather?"

"Ah, you know. General disruption. Gettin' calls all night. People in a fuss to get bread and milk for fear they'll be stuck indoors for eternity on account of the storm and all. Things get out of hand, people start fighting', bein' rowdy. Can't stand to be cooped up for too long, I guess. We get all sorts of calls. Pranks, even. One came in a few hours ago, screamin' about a crazy person running around these parts shootin' people with a shotgun, killin' her friends or something along those lines."

Samantha.

Ted knew it immediately. He didn't know what the state trooper knew, but he knew it couldn't have been anyone else. Samantha tried to call for help, and there was help, sitting totally oblivious to the fact that they needed it.

Ted felt his heart beating overtime. Felt the taste of freedom on the tip of his tongue. It was only a matter of time—a matter of moments before all of this was over. The state trooper would see what was going on and would take this man away, Samantha would come back upstairs; they would get in the Jeep and drive as far from there as they could.

It was when Ted spied the box-cutter behind Michael's back, still held firm in his grip, ready to strike, that he remembered who held the leverage. Michael still had the upper hand. And he wasn't going out without a fight.

They could try to jump him, but the distance made it too much of a risk. They could yell at the trooper and tell him what was going on, that they were being held prisoner, but Ted harbored no doubts that if put in a place with no exit, Michael would drag that rusted old blade across Julia's neck that very instant, not a second thought on the matter. The man had nothing left to lose.

"Ridiculous stuff, Mike," Lou said, "But it's my job to come out and poke around, make sure everything's well."

"Yeah, everything is well. Everything's great, all things considered."

"Good to hear that. Say—where's Carla? I hope she's not out there drivin' around in this mess."

"No, she's staying at her sister's place. Safer than trying to drive home."

It was a lie, but a good one, Ted thought. And it came to Michael quick, as if he'd been thinking about it. Planning for it. Always thinking one step ahead, considering every circumstance, leaving nothing to chance.

"That's good of her. Giver her my good graces when you see her, Mike." Lou rose to his feet and stretched. "Are you sure you're okay, young lady?"

"I'm fine," Julia said. Looking at her, though, it was obvious she was in a great deal of discomfort.

"I could call for an ambulance, Mike. They'd be out

here in less than half an hour."

"No, you don't have to do that. She's just feeling under the weather."

"You sure? It's really no biggie…"

"Yeah. No need to put lives at risk for something so minor." Michael stood, moved a few feet closer to Lou while discreetly clipping the open box-cutter to the back pocket of his jeans. "That story about the … the shotgun. Are you sure that's just a story?"

Lou nodded a big, hearty, confident nod. "Well, you never know anything until you see it with your own eyes, but sounds pretty far-fetched to me."

"You know, because if someone was out there while we're stuck in here… These kids would feel a lot safer knowing it was just a joke. Did you get a name?"

"A name?" Lou asked.

"Whoever placed the call," Michael said. "Did they give a name?"

Lou shook his head. "Nope, don't think they ever did. Now, I didn't hear the call for myself, but they pulled a name from the caller ID. Sally something… Sandy, Suzie… Began with an S… Sammy—Samantha! That was it. Samantha something or other. Heck, I'm lucky I can remember my own name half the time!" He finished with a laugh and a pat against Michael's arm.

"We'll let you know if we hear anything else," Michael said.

"Thanks, Mike. But you know… I'm going to call an ambulance for this young lady. She doesn't look very well to me."

Michael put a hand on Lou's shoulder. "No, no, that's really unnecessary—"

"Ah, it just wouldn't be Christian of me to leave her here like this." Lou's hand started up toward the radio mic clipped to his uniform shoulder.

"Lou, it's really not necessary. Look, the storm is getting worse and I don't want you getting stuck out there if it gets as bad as they say it is."

Lou stepped closer to speak quietly to Michael. "I'm not a doctor, but I know when someone's in pain when I see it, and I see it as plain as the day is long. That young girl's hurtin', Mike."

Michael sucked a deep breath as Lou let a moment of understanding pass between them.

Ted's attention hung on their every word, now stretching out to unbearable lengths as those words stopped and an uncomfortable silence crept in. Thunder boomed close by, and a blink of lightning followed.

The weather *was* getting worse, he realized. With Samantha making an appearance and all that followed, the thought of keeping up with the weather reports on the silenced TV came nowhere close to crossing Ted's mind. But he knew the rush of rainfall was ever-present. The sound hadn't left his ears alone.

Then he saw Lou's hand make another move for the radio mic, but this time is was impeded. By Michael's own hand.

"I don't think that's a good idea," Michael said, looking Lou straight in the eyes.

Lou flashed a look that fell between dismay and concern. "Mike, just sit down and let me handle this." He turned his head to Julia. "This'll take just two seconds, miss."

Lou's hand finally found itself on the radio mic.

He never saw the blade coming.

SEVENTEEN

IN ONE STROKE, THE radio cable and Lou's carotid artery were both severed.

The amputated mic fell from Lou's deadened fingers. His knees slammed into the floor and his body slumped over with a disturbing thud, sending up an arc of arterial spray that bathed Julia, the couch, the wall, the floor, and everything nearby in a crimson mist.

Ted's jaw hung open in disbelief. Their ticket home was now writhing like a crippled insect, choking to death on his own blood from the wound that Michael inflicted. Not on a stranger, but a man who had known him on a first-name basis.

This was the moment, Ted realized definitively, that they were not making it out of that house alive.

Bobby had sensed it, too. One whiff of the opportunity and he took it—leaping from his seat while Michael was distracted.

But Bobby was halted almost as quickly as he had begun when he saw the state trooper's sidearm held in Michael's grasp, trained on him.

No words needed to be said for Bobby to return to his seat. He kept one eye on the gun and the other on Julia, who now sat upright, stirred wide awake. She raised trembling hands to wipe the blood from her face, eyes wide with horror. Looking at the rest of her body, also stained with the blood of the state trooper, was too much.

Ted had never before seen fear in Julia Thisbe. This was the girl who grabbed life by the throat and fought it every single day, even when it fought back harder. Especially then. But now, turning her eyes on Bobby, Ted saw a look he would never forget. It was a look of everything she knew, everything she was, every hope and dream, gone. There was emptiness inside her.

Michael dropped the box-cutter in favor of the more threatening handgun. He ran his bloody hand through his hair, staring in the direction of Ted and Bobby.

He was calm, Ted noticed. Far too calm. The state trooper's breathing had slowed to a stop, but Michael's chest was rising and falling in the rhythm of an innocent man. Ted knew any attempt at reasoning with this person was out of the question from here on.

Michael lowered the Glock 21 .45ACP. "Who the fuck is Samantha?"

Nobody knew how to answer.

"Speak up. Who is Samantha? You know her," Michael said, making sure they knew the last part was not a question.

"I don't know," Ted said. He knew Michael was smart enough to see through the lie, but remaining silent would seem like more of an admission of guilt. And it would only serve to further infuriate a man with all the leverage and nothing to lose.

A smirk formed in the corner of Michael's mouth. He was lacking patience. From the coffee table, he grabbed one of the three cell phones and looked in its contact list. His thumb scrolled down until he found what he was looking for. He turned the evidence on the screen toward Ted and Bobby. "Samantha Millner. Know her?"

It was too far away to see what was on the screen, but it was certainly Julia's phone. Samantha's number had been added the day before. Ted had thought it was a good idea that everyone could get in touch with everyone else in the event of an emergency during the vacation. He wasn't thinking the same thing now.

Michael hit the touch-screen with a finger and held the phone to his ear.

Ted waited for the sound of Samantha's ring-tone—a marimba piece with an island vibe. She'd kept the same one for as far back as Ted could remember. He knew every note. Sometimes he would find it annoying in its familiarity and its tendency to get lodged in his head for hours on end; other times it was an endearing example of what made Samantha who she was, being able to instill her own identity into everything that belonged to her, even the small things that other people would overlook or take for granted.

It was the tiny moments that Ted found so endearing. Samantha saw love everywhere, it seemed. Nothing was exempt, big or small. She found the things she liked most and held on to them. Maybe she didn't see that in herself, but Ted knew it was there.

But now it wasn't the island percussion Ted was hearing; a silence haunted his thoughts, urged on by the droning wail as the rain outside fell through the wind, screaming down to saturate the fields and farmland.

Michael hung up the phone almost immediately. It

had gone straight to voice mail. Either the phone was off or the battery had died. Or it was still charging in the car. Ted had no idea, but what he did know was that Samantha was nearby. And he was thankful the call did not go through. The last thing he wanted to hear in that moment was that damn marimba.

Michael swooped down to pick up another phone— Bobby's. He threw it aside after getting no further than the lock screen. Without warning, he fired a bullet into each phone on the floor, and another into Ted's that still sat on the coffee table. Three cannon-blasts that rocked the room in quick succession.

Ted felt the force of each shot reverberating in the center of his chest. He heard nothing for several seconds, then only a high-end ringing. Seeing the gun in his enemy's hand was bad enough, but hearing what it could do terrified Ted to his very core. The shotgun didn't seem to have the same effect with its limited capacity and hindered mobility, but this new weapon had a bullet for everyone in the house.

"Where is she?" Michael's voice sounded distant, as if speaking through a cloud, but it was only the effects of the gunshots on Ted's hearing.

"I don't know," said Ted. This time, he only told half a lie.

"You had the only vehicle that showed up, so she must have ridden with you." Michael raised the gun. "Where is she? Where did she go?"

Michael was careful to stay at the other end of the room, close enough to Julia that any thoughts Bobby or Ted would have of mounting an offensive were dead on arrival—but still close enough to hit his target should that not be the case.

"She never made it out of the Jeep," Ted said. That was close enough to the truth. Samantha had made it out of the Jeep, but in her haste to exit, she had slipped in the mud and fell—blessedly out of Michael's view.

Ted wondered how badly she hurt herself. In the seconds she stood in front of him before sliding the box-cutter across the floor and disappearing, it did not look good. She might have cracked a rib, bruised an internal organ… It wasn't something Ted wanted to think about. He had to keep his mind clear. Poor judgment would not get them out of that house.

"I drove it around the house and she wasn't inside. Where did she go?" Michael asked, as if Ted would know the answer.

"No clue. I was in here the whole time."

"Then you must have seen who gave that one the knife," Michael said, pointing to Bobby. "He didn't pull it out of his ass, so where did it come from?"

Ted was too frightened to speak. What could he say? He wasn't about to give Samantha up, but there was no other choice.

Michael's finger waved accusations between Ted and Bobby. "You're hiding something from me, and I don't like that. That girl is in this house, isn't she?"

Only the wind and rain responded.

"Fine. If you want to do it the hard way…" Michael turned, grabbed a fistful of Julia's hair, and yanked her down to the floor. She landed in the state trooper's blood with a cry of anguish.

Bobby was on his feet that second, and Michael's gun was on Bobby. "Go ahead, hot shot," Michael said. It was an obvious taunt meant to provoke.

"You want to pick a fight, pick one with me," Bobby said, his voice hot with animal instincts. There was blood in the air.

"I already did," Michael said. "And I won."

Bobby fumed. Ted saw the look in his eye and thought he was going to rush Michael at a moment's notice. Julia was the only thing holding him back.

Michael spoke to where Julia lay at his feet. "Call to her."

Julia wormed her way onto her side, trying to get to her knees, but her wounded body would not allow it. Strands of blood-soaked hair stuck to her face. Her arms were slick and red, weak hands working against the crimson spill beneath her.

She refused to look at Michael.

"I said call to her." Michael held the sidearm in the direction of the two men across the room, keeping them in place.

No words came from Julia's labored breaths.

"Maybe you need a little incentive…" Michael fell to a crouch and worked the engagement ring from Julia's finger. He stood, holding the ring out for Bobby to see through the fire in his eyes.

One flick of the wrist and the ring soared through the stagnant heat of the living room and out of view, clinking against the kitchen tiles before coming to rest.

Bobby was set to explode. It was only a matter of time. The fuse had been lit. Ted wasn't sure his friend could take much more abuse. Physically, Bobby could stand up to any force, and if it managed to knock him down, he would pick himself right back up. But mentally… He could snap at any time. Ted had seen Bobby when he was angry before, and it wasn't good for the other person.

Michael held the upper hand and the state trooper's gun within it. Bobby had to think about self-preservation and that of his soon-to-be wife, Julia. The ring yanked from her finger, there was no telling what steps Michael would take next. Bobby had to call out to Samantha.

"Samantha's not here," Bobby said. "I don't know where she is, but she's long gone."

Displeasure crossed Michael's face. He gave the look of a man who didn't like to be jerked around. "Long gone? Well then… I guess you'll just have to *speak up*—"

Ted saw Michael's size-eleven work boot drift back in slow motion and then swing forward with uncompromising menace, driving into the small of Julia's back.

A wail of bloody-murder consumed the living room.

Ted leaped from his seat to restrain Bobby as best as he could, but his average build against Bobby's blind fury was no match. Bobby shrugged Ted aside and charged for Julia's assailant.

Another gunshot rang out and Bobby dropped instantly as he bled from a bullet wound in his shoulder.

The chaos of sounds drowned out the violence of the storm. Bobby groaned as he tried to stand. Julia moaned; the pain had her mouth frozen in a silent scream. Ted's ears rang again.

"*Stop!*"

The voice found its way through the mess and into a place where Ted knew whom it belonged to. It cut through everything else that was going on, drawing the attention of not only Ted, but Michael.

Heads turned to the doorway that separated the kitchen from the living room, to the petite figure, sullen, a picture of ruin that stood with trembling hands raised in surrender.

"Please," Samantha said, the word coming out weak and frail, "Please don't hurt my friends."

EIGHTEEN

"ARE YOU SAMANTHA?"

She nodded, eyes cast down, too afraid to meet Michael's stone-cold stare.

"Samantha Millner? The one who called the cops?" His words were backed by winds and thunder.

Her jaw quivered and tears filled her eyes, rolling down her dirty face. Michael stormed to where Samantha stood, grabbed her by the arm and threw her to the floor. She fell on her hands and knees, inches from the state trooper's body.

"Do you see that?" Michael bent over and clasped a muscular hand around the back of her neck, forcing her to stare at the dead man's lacerated throat. "This is all your fault!" His voice boomed with an intensity not seen or heard before. "Look what you made me do!"

Michael shoved Samantha's face against the bloody wound and held it there for the longest second before letting go.

Samantha gagged, spitting the blood out of her mouth and nose. She wiped it from her face, away from her eyes. It was still on her lips; she could taste it. Her stomach felt weak, bile rising in the back of her throat.

All she wanted to do was throw up. Let everything out, right here and right now. Purge her body of every negative thing swimming around inside her, in her stomach, in her head, wherever it may be. The weight of everything she was responsible for was squeezing the life from her. It was a weight she could not lift.

Samantha choked out more bloody spit. The retched ball in her gut would not relent, writhing inside her like a venomous parasite clawing for escape. She could still taste the blood of the man she called upon; it was on her tongue, between her teeth, sliming its way down the constricted passage of her throat.

This is all your fault, Samantha. All your fault. You killed this man. You brought him here and you killed him.

That internal voice surrounded her every thought, and she knew it was right. This man would still be alive if she'd never made that call. If her phone battery died before she was able to get through to someone. If she took a chance on running away and finding help in person, explaining the gravity of the situation. Any number of things could have happened that kept the state trooper from arriving, but none of them did happen.

Samantha rolled upright and scampered back against the couch. Before her, whimpering in sheer agony was Julia, face down, jaw clenched so tight that Samantha was sure her teeth were going to shatter. A thin line of drool hung from the corner of her mouth, pooling on the hardwood below.

This was all your fault, Samantha. All your fault.

They had never been the closest friends, but seeing Julia in this state broke Samantha down. It felt as though someone had driven a spike through her heart. *It wasn't supposed to be like this*, she thought to herself. They were supposed to be on the road, driving, listening to music together, joking and laughing. Far away from here. They were never supposed to come here.

Samantha tried to look away, but her eyes seemed unable to find a sight that wasn't unsettling. Julia on the floor, frozen in anguish; Bobby crawling to her, bullet wound bleeding in his shoulder; Michael towering above them with the state trooper's gun in hand.

Samantha couldn't bring herself to look at Ted. She didn't want him to see her like this. Dirty, covered in filth from head to toe, her hair a knotted disaster, a stranger's blood smeared on her tearstained face. She wanted to be strong, but this is not what a strong person looked like. This was weakness.

But even with her head turned away, Samantha felt Ted's eyes on her. She felt his concern. Felt his presence. She felt … something else. Not within herself, but in Ted. It was an impulse. He was always a rational thinker, never erratic. Always careful.

Samantha had no idea how she knew what was about to happen. Like the odd times when friends are able to finish each other's sentences, know what the other is thinking before they say it, connected on a deeper level… Samantha knew Ted wanted the state trooper's gun.

As much as she wanted to turn her eyes to meet his, shake her head in disagreement, shout, scream and yell for him to not take the chance, there was no other option Samantha could think of. She tried to be smart—and she was, for the most part. Tried to keep quiet, out of sight. Do everything she could to help, to keep her friends and herself safe. Her efforts brought them all to this point. It wasn't what she wished for. Not what she anticipated. There had to be something they could do. Another option of some sort. But if Ted, now void of reason, was thinking about making a break for the gun, Samantha knew their alternatives had truly been exhausted.

Michael paced back and forth, his fingers tight around the firearm's grip, index finger sweating on the trigger. There was a rage in his eyes, pouring from every line in his face. He watched Bobby comfort Julia. He watched Ted sitting across the room. He watched Samantha, who sat with arms crossed and knees pulled up, her eyes averted. He watched everything and nothing.

High winds and torrential rainfall battered the exterior of the home. Michael's head swiveled to catch a glimpse out a window overlooking the front porch. Lightning struck less than a mile away, and thunder answered before the flash was through.

It was just enough of a distraction.

Footsteps flew across the living room floor. Samantha had never seen Ted move so fast. Michael spun at the sound, but, leaping through the air, Ted was on him before he had a chance to react.

The force drove Michael stumbling back, two bodies colliding against the wall mere inches from the window. The gun was raised. Ted grabbed the wrist with two hands and slammed the weapon against the glass.

The fingers held firm.

Ted threw all his weight into the next slam. Glass shattered. Storm winds invaded the living room of the home. Rain beat against everything, spilling in through the broken window. The glass broke outward then flew inward in an onrush of leaves, dirt and debris.

But the fingers held firm.

Samantha found herself on her feet. She scanned the area for a weapon, anything she could use to help. Then it hit her—the screwdriver she'd had in her back pocket the whole time. Before she could reach her hand around, Bobby rushed past and jumped into the fray.

Together, Ted and Bobby wrestled against Michael's grip on the gun, driving his arm downward, the jagged teeth of shattered glass reaching up to greet him. The strength of two was not something Michael could overpower. His arm came down, pierced by the transparent spire that jutted out of the window frame. A red stain spilled down the glass, but then it was gone, washed away by the incoming rainfall, dripping to the floor in a pink puddle.

Michael let out a groan as the spike of window ripped through his flesh like a razor blade, severing tendons and muscle tissue with shocking ease. His hand opened, fingers yawning back and taking the weapon with them.

Ted caught the state trooper's sidearm before it had a chance to fall out of the window into the wet and screaming darkness. He backed away, leaving no room for Michael to reach out or leap for the upper hand without taking a bullet wound for his efforts. He was using Michael's own trick against him.

Bobby rushed back to Julia's side, stroking her hair, telling her everything would be alright. Her fingernails clawed against the hardwood. She was in a daze somewhere beyond consciousness.

The sooner they left, the better, Samantha thought. No sense in hanging around any longer. She expected to be flooded by a profound relief now that freedom was in their grasp, but she stood on edge. Seeing Michael standing there, blood seeping from between his fingers as he held pressure against his lacerated arm, a sick smile twisted across his face… It was a sight that brought no repose.

Only now did she turn to look into Ted's eyes, but Ted did not return the look. He kept his focus trained forward, following the aim of the gun barrel to the center of Michael's chest. No chance he would allow himself to make the same mistake as Michael. If they wanted to leave this place alive, they had to be smarter than Michael, more careful than him.

"What are you gonna do?" Michael taunted. "Shoot me?" His lips were still contorted in a grimace faintly resembling a smirk. It was the look of a man at the end of his rope. The look of a man who had everything just hours ago but now held nothing. His life was slipping away, piece by piece. First his farm, if the broken sign in the basement was any indication. Then his wife, taking with her all the years of passion and loyalty they had shared. Now his home was under attack, and his sanity was fading fast.

Ted thought about how to answer. Samantha could see his mind working, contemplating every moment from here on, leaving nothing to chance. "Maybe," he said.

"Then do it. Why wait? Just get it over with."

Samantha somehow felt more tension than she had when Michael held the weapon. Now the decisions were in her hands, and the hands of her friends. In Ted's hands. She knew their actions now had consequences that went beyond themselves. They were involving the life of another human being, and no doubt questioning whether or not to take it.

"Ted, we need to go," Samantha said. She had to speak

up. Someone had to alleviate the stress in the air.

"I know." Ted's eyes held firm on Michael, but his words went to Samantha.

"She's right," Bobby called from behind. "We have to get Julia to a hospital." He said nothing about his own wounds.

Their talk seemed to kindle the manic glow behind Michael's eyes. "What are you gonna do, Ted," he said in mocking tones.

Against all impulse, Samantha maintained her gaze on Ted. Her eyes bore into him, trying to see what he was thinking, what he was going to do next. Trying to see the good, kind-hearted man she had such powerful feelings for. A man of reason and understanding. A man incapable of killing. She didn't want to look within Ted and see him corrupted in the way that Michael had been.

Though terrified of what she might see, Samantha refused to look away.

She could see it in Ted's eyes, his mind working fast, weighing possibilities, gauging solutions.

A red and blue swirl of light strafed through the living room, dim from the drawn curtains. The state trooper's vehicle was still outside.

"Samantha," said Ted.

She froze where she stood. Her blood turned to ice.

"Inside the car out front there is a radio," Ted said. The grimace on his face told that he hated himself for what he was about to ask. "I need you to use it to call for help."

Samantha's joints froze. She stood like a statue, not wishing to go back outside and into the storm. She had already been stranded outside in the elements. Alone. Hurt. But their options were limited. Julia couldn't move. Bobby wouldn't leave her side. Someone had to hold Michael in check, and with an injured shoulder, Bobby couldn't handle the crazed and unpredictable murderer on his own.

Ted's voice cut through Samantha's mental fog. "Samantha, listen to me. You have to do this."

She knew Ted couldn't take the chance of letting his focus on Michael slip—not even for half a second. Michael was too smart. Worse, he was unstable. He may not wait for Ted's attention to falter before making a dive for the gun.

Samantha bit both her lips. She turned terrified eyes to Ted. "I…I don't…"

"Please. Samantha, there's no one else."

"Ted, I…"

Ted just listened, eyes on Michael, who remained pressed against the wall and clutching his bleeding forearm.

This is it, girl. This is your chance. Nobody is going to do it for you. It has to be you.

Samantha looked around, from Ted to Julia to Bobby. They were all counting on her. No matter how much she disliked the idea of running outside into the very storm that had brought them to that fateful farmhouse, she had to do it. She had to find the will to keep going, to go further, go where her sister would have gone.

You can do it, Samantha.

"Okay," she said in a shallow voice. "I'll go."

Ted sighed in relief. "The keys should still be inside. Make it *fast*."

Ted didn't need to mention the storm coverage on television for Samantha to know the weather outside was intensifying. She could see it in the way the winds howled in through the broken window, casting blown leaves and

NINETEEN

THROUGH THE WIND AND RAIN, Samantha ran, bathed in red and blue lights perpetually flashing on the state trooper's vehicle, as though they were a silent bell tolling for the deceased.

Her feet picked up mud and leaves as she made for the driver's door. She swung it open, threw herself inside, and slammed it shut.

She gazed around, temporarily mesmerized by all the controls before her. She felt like a cop just then, with the weight of human life pressing down on her. On the center console, she found the police radio.

"Hello? Hello, anyone?"

The silence she heard felt eternal. Nobody was going to answ—

"Unit 17, please identify."

Samantha nearly dropped the hand control as the voice crackled through a signal plagued by static. "This is Samantha. The officer is dead. Please send help. Please, it's not safe here."

Static crackled again like an alien transmission attempting to break through, stuck at an invisible barrier.

"Hello? Is anyone there," Samantha cried into the radio.

Silence.

The front door sprang open and Samantha flew inside, slamming it shut to keep the storm from following.

Ted didn't look away from Michael. "Did you get anyone?"

Samantha choked out deep breaths. "It's all static. I don't know if they heard me."

Ted didn't have to say the word *shit* out loud. Samantha knew he had said it to himself as his plans slipped through his fingertips.

Bobby extended his hand to Ted, palm-up. "Come on, Ted. We can't stand here like this all night."

Samantha's gaze darted between them two young men, unsure of what had happened in her absence. She peeled her wet hair from her face with one hand, keeping the other against her ribs. She moved behind Ted, putting space between her and Michael.

Ted maintained his grip on the gun and his aim on Michael. "What's that supposed to mean?"

Bobby scoffed. "We're just gonna drive away and let this guy go? No way."

"There has to be another way out of this," Ted said with carefully-chosen words, as if he didn't want to upset anyone any more than they already were. Openly discussing murder wasn't going to do them any favors.

"I can think of one," Bobby said.

Samantha realized that Bobby's mind had also been made up. He wasn't about to let the attack on Julia go unpunished.

Ted's chest rose and fell heavily. "Well, think of a few more so you're sure we're doing the right thing."

Were they doing the right thing? The thought haunted

Samantha's conscience. Shooting a defenseless man was murder, but after what he did to a total stranger, to his own wife, and a state trooper… They couldn't just drive off and let the man go free, nor could they tie him up in the midst of this storm. He could die if anything happened to the house, or starve if nobody found him in time. Putting a bullet in his chest was, frighteningly, the more humane option.

But there was another thing to consider: they were the only witnesses.

There was a chance, Samantha thought, that if they drive off and left this man here, he could blame the deaths on two young men and two young women who passed through. It was a remote possibility, but Michael was intelligent enough to spin it in a way that made sense to the authorities. A couple of spree-killers fleeing across the country. After gunning down a state trooper, they'd be shot on sight. If not by the police, then by any one of the locals who knew the man by name, as Michael had.

Samantha shook the thought away. She couldn't believe what she was thinking. She was letting herself get lost in the possibilities instead of recognizing the paths that would end this standoff.

"Ted?" Samantha said. She left the question hang.

Though he didn't turn his head away from Michael, Ted seemed to know what she wanted to ask. *Can we go home?* It was in the shiver in her voice, in the way she stood behind him, silently asking for protection, for a way out of this home and a safe passage back to her own.

Samantha didn't know the extent of Julia's injuries, but she knew it was bad. The strongest person she had ever met was lying in defeat, unable to stand. Samantha wasn't sure there was even a safe way to move her into a vehicle to escape.

Something at that moment clicked in Ted. Samantha caught the subtle movement of his shoulders, the restrained desire to spin around and look her in the eye. A sudden realization, something he couldn't believe he didn't think of until just then. "Samantha, was there a cage in the car?"

"Yes," she said. "There was. In the back."

That was it. That was their answer. "Okay," Ted said to Michael, "this is how things are going to go. You walk outside, climb in the back seat, and close the door."

Michael laughed. "Oh, really? That's what's going to happen?"

"Your choice."

"That's as good as killing me right here. There's tornado warnings all over the county. Look at the TV."

Ted almost fell for it. A clever distraction, one Ted no doubt felt compelled to investigate. It was true that the storm was intensifying. It had been all night. Tornado warnings were not surprising, but nevertheless a caution they had to heed. "Bend over and hand me the keys."

Michael's hand shifted to his back pocket. "You may want your own keys back, first."

Samantha hadn't realized that Michael still had the keys to the Jeep. Nor had she realized that when Michael's hand emerged from his pocket, it was not holding any keys.

Before anyone had a chance to react, Samantha tasted the foul burning of the state trooper's pepper spray as Michael blasted it into Ted's eyes in front of her.

TWENTY

TED CRIED OUT AND FELL to his knees, his hands pressed firm against his eyes. The next sound Samantha heard was the clatter of the state trooper's sidearm as it escaped Ted's grasp and hit the floor.

What happened after that seemed impossibly fast. The gun was back in Michael's hand, and a shot rang out. A body dropped with the weight of the dead, collapsing next to Julia.

Samantha found her hands covering her mouth, a scream stifled in the back of her throat. She barely even knew Bobby Welliver, they were scarcely friends, barely talked, but her heart ached just the same.

This is all my fault. I killed him. I caused all of this.
This is my punishment.

Samantha's only thought was to run. It's what she should have done in the first place. Run away from here, away to where you can't be harmed. Where you can't cause anyone harm. Run for help. Run. Just run and keep running.

Her legs didn't want to move, trained throughout the whole ordeal to stay rooted in place. She had to struggle to make the first step, but everything came easy after that initial effort. She found herself in motion, crossing the living room, stepping over the fallen, running to safety.

But her flight would not last long.

A set of rough fingers pulled at her upper arm, their grip like a vice, as strong as the machines out on the storm-tossed farm. Samantha felt her momentum suddenly shift, the inertia jarring her in body and mind. She tried to wrench herself free from the hand clamped on her arm, but the world suddenly went silent as a pain shot through her skull, piercing from one temple to the other, and then everything was quiet.

Images faded into amorphous blurs. Indistinct. Random. A rush of sound swelled inside Samantha's head, akin to that of the rainfall, but that was outside; what she heard was within her. She wanted to panic, but couldn't find the energy. It was as if the blow had drained her of her very will to escape, imprisoning her in the idea that closing her eyes and resting was all she could do now, was all that she needed.

The strange shapes slowly took form. Samantha blinked, then blinked again. Her vision was returning. Staring her in the face was the pointed edge of the coffee table. She raised a hand to her temple and felt fresh blood moisten the dirt on her fingertips.

Though images were now clear, the room felt unsteady, as if shaken by the storm. Samantha pictured the entirety of the farmhouse floating and twisting and tumbling about in the center of a giant tornado. This was surely what that would feel like.

Pushing aside the dull throb in her skull, Samantha raised her head over the coffee table, terrified of what was waiting for her.

Across the room, Michael was crouched, working at something at the base of the radiator. She didn't see Ted's face, but she knew it was him. It had to be. There was nobody else now.

Samantha found the impulse to run as strong as ever. There was nothing she could do to save Ted. There were no weapons she could grab. There were no others to help her. She had only one option.

Get out of here.

She planted a hand on the coffee table and one of her feet against the floor. The moment she had Ted in her sights, their eyes locked, and an agreement was reached. Unspoken, but delivered. She saw it in his bloodshot eyes, a look she had never seen before. Helplessness. Defeat. Fear.

From that one look, Samantha knew what he wanted her to do.

She wanted to stay and help. She wanted to do something. All she had done on this day was make bad situations worse.

Ted snapped alert as Michael turned his focus across the living room to where Samantha knelt, frozen with one hand on the table and one foot on the floor, halfway between lying down and sprinting away.

"Samantha, *run!*"

It was no longer the impulse telling her. It was now Ted himself yelling in his own words. A simple command. She knew it was her only option. They both knew. He didn't want her to put herself in harm's way any longer. As badly as Samantha wished to be of some help, she knew she was not her sister. She had to run. It was all she could do.

"He doesn't have the gun! GO!"

Michael was on his feet first, moving at her from a

deliberate angle, cutting off her path to the front door. Samantha pulled herself up and backed away. Michael advanced, pushing her away from the exits, blocking her from retreating. There was only one way to go…

Samantha turned and sprinted up the stairs to the second floor.

She had no idea what she was thinking. *This isn't a way out, this is a trap.* But it was better than standing her ground against Michael. She would rather engage in a battle of wits than a battle of fists. He had the foresight to steal the state trooper's pepper spray before he needed it, grabbing it from the man's belt as another victim of the night fell to the floor to die. He was prepared enough to pressure her into a corner instead of allowing her to leave the house.

Without the gun, there was a chance she could do something, find something, a weapon, anything upstairs in the dark. Something to push him down the stairs, bash him over the head with.

Why didn't he have the gun? Something happened in her daze, a struggle between Ted and Michael. Ted must have wrestled it away, but… *Where is it now?* That was the weapon Samantha had to find. She knew it wasn't upstairs, but if she could find a way to hide, some way of getting lost in the dark so Michael couldn't find her, she thought maybe—just maybe—she could circle around him and sneak down to the first floor.

Samantha strained to see through the pitch black of the second floor hallway. No lights were on, only the faint glow that started at the base of the steps and faded into nothing before reaching the top. The pain in her head poked like a thorn every time she blinked.

She told herself to keep calm. She was not hurt as badly as she thought. She didn't feel dizzy or nauseated, just a bit foggy. Foggy, she could deal with. She had grown used to the pain in her side; it was still present, however, and she knew that was not a good thing.

She shuffled in baby-steps, fumbling hands drawn out before her, waiting to find ... something. She walked her hands along the nearest wall until they happened upon what felt like the knob of a door. She gave it a turn, hoping the sound wouldn't carry, praying this old, creaky farmhouse would do her this one simple favor.

A bolt of lightning lent half of a second of light, and within that half of a second, Samantha saw the edges of the door frame. She swung herself around the half-opened door and was in before the thunderclap had sounded.

Backing away from the door, Samantha bumped into something soft. The end of a bed? Her eyes were beginning to adjust and the cloud of fog inside her head was growing thin, but it was still too dark to make out anything for certain. It felt like a bed; that's all she knew.

If this was a bedroom, there would be a closet. If not, she could duck under the bed, and...

Dammit, Samantha! Is that really your best idea?

Alice always found her when she hid under the bed, and when she hid in the closet, too. If there truly was skill involved in hide-and-seek, it was lost on Samantha. She couldn't outsmart a child; how could she hope to pull a fast one on this intelligent grown man?

A light clicked on in the hallway just beyond the bedroom door, seeping in from the little space between the door and the floor.

Samantha's eyes fell into that little space, watching and

waiting for two shadows cast by a pair of dirty work boots to appear on the other side.

Her heart was pounding. Her head was pounding. She felt ill. She wanted to scream, cry, fight. But she couldn't do anything. She couldn't even see. The darkness was no longer a friend to her. A friend would reach out, take her by the hand, and show her the way home.

The darkness was cast out as the bedroom door opened in a groan of old hinges, a sound that had no end. But it wasn't the sound that chilled the very marrow of her bones … it was the silhouette of the man standing in the doorway.

TWENTY-ONE

THE CABLE TIES WERE CUTTING off circulation to Ted's wrists. If he could see his hands, he would expect them to be purple by now.

His eyes still burned. He had never been pepper-sprayed before, but whatever was in that little bottle was no joke. His eyes watered as if he had spent the day crying. Runny snot dripped from his nose. Even the back of his throat burned.

Though half-blinded, he was able to make out the dark shape of Michael's figure moving about in the Technicolor glow of the old-timey television set. The sound of heavy footsteps crossed the floor and climbed the squeaking steps one at a time. They appeared to be in no hurry at all.

If there was a time to hurry, it was now, Ted decided. He wrestled against the cable ties that held both wrists to the base of the radiator to the point where he felt blood dripping onto his hands and fingers.

"Shit!" It was hopeless. He was going to cut himself to the point of bleeding to death if he wasn't able to break through the cable ties. Even the smallest ones were a pain in the ass, but the larger, thicker grade that strangled the blood supply to his hands seemed impossible to escape.

"Ted…"

He didn't expect anyone to answer his obscenity, but he was floored with relief when he heard Julia's voice, low and withered under the droning wind and rain.

"Julia, are you okay?"

What kind of question was that? Ted felt stupid for even asking, but it was the first thing that came to mind. *No. Shit. She's not okay.*

"Ted… I…" She tried for more words, but only tears came.

"Julia, listen. Are you listening?" He had to make sure she was cognizant of what was going on around her. If she was in any kind of mental or emotional stupor, Ted knew he would not find support.

"Yes."

"There should be a knife on the floor nearby. The box-cutter." Ted thought he caught a glimpse of it near the coffee table, but his attention was too focused on Michael to be positive. And he still couldn't see worth a damn.

The only sound Ted heard was the storm blowing in through the shattered window on the opposite side of the living room.

"Julia, please. Look around and tell me if you see it."

Moments passed before Julia replied. Agonizing moments. "I see it."

"Where?"

"Just under the table."

Ted was right. He knew he'd seen that knife. And if memory served, Julia couldn't be more than three feet from it. He drew a deep breath. "Julia, I don't want to have to ask you this, but I need you to see if you can reach it."

"Ted…" She wanted to say more, but couldn't bring

herself to utter the words.

He knew by the emotion in her voice that the answer was no. "Julia, please."

"I can't. I can't do it." Every syllable was choked with tears.

Ted was stunned. Of all the people he had ever known, the last one who would say "I can't" was Julia Thisbe. She had overcome so much in her life, but this was it. This was the moment where she gave up.

"Julia, don't say that. You're the strongest person I know, and I need you to be strong right now. Can you be strong for me?"

Everyone has a breaking point, Ted thought. Michael had reached his when he found his wife with another man. Surely, Michael had not awoken that morning thinking he was ever capable of the deeds he was going to commit. Ted had certainly not awoken that morning expecting to find himself imprisoned in a stranger's living room with his best friends either dead or fighting for their lives.

Ted tried not to think of the deeds he was capable of once his breaking point was reached.

Julia breathed measured breaths. It felt to Ted that she was working up the strength—both physically and mentally—to make an effort to grab the box-cutter.

Maybe she had not given up. Maybe she just needed someone to remind her of who she was. No matter how strong you are, everyone needs a push in one way or another from time to time. Maybe Julia was incapable of giving up. She just needed a push.

"I know you can do it, Julia. You're strong. You can totally do this." Ted thought with enough motivation, she could possibly reach it. It was a long way to go for a person who could barely move.

Julia reached out one arm and slammed her palm into the floor. Then her other hand slammed down. Ted could hear her fighting back screams of anguish. Even now, in this wildest of circumstances, she didn't want to appear weak.

It was a stroke of good fortune, Ted knew, Michael leaving the box-cutter on the floor. He had not made many mistakes, so this seemed out of character for a man who took so many precautionary measures to maintain the upper hand. There was the possibility that he wanted Ted to get free, not satisfied with an easy kill.

That was far-fetched. Michael had simply screwed up. He had only dropped the knife upon taking possession of the state trooper's gun, which Ted was fortunate enough to kick down the basement stairs. In a blind scuffle, Ted swung a wild foot based only on the sounds he had heard - the gun falling at their feet, bouncing aside. He knew the direction of the door Samantha had left open and took a shot.

Ted drew another calming breath. This was the first moment he had realized just how lucky he was to be alive. If not for his lunge at Michael that stripped him of the gun, he would almost certainly be dead. Julia and Samantha as well.

Julia squeezed her fingernails into the slivers of space where two boards met and pulled herself forward using only her upper-body strength. Ted heard the whimpers of suffering, no matter how hard she tried to stifle them.

"How close are you?"

Julia had to catch her breath before answering. "Almost…"

The box-cutter couldn't have been more than two feet from where she lay. This much effort to move two feet…

Ted felt a pang of shame for ever posing the question. Julia was hurt, and hurt bad, but she was the only option. There was no chance of Ted reaching it himself. Not unless he was willing to risk losing a hand or at least a good slab of flesh in the process.

He had a vague plan for if and when he cut himself free, but there was no outline for how to get Julia out of here safely. He had been chewing it over ever since he first held the gun in his hands. He couldn't risk picking her up and injuring her further, and waiting for an ambulance in this weather was not wise.

The house shook against the strong winds. Smaller items were falling over every other minute. The very walls themselves creaked and groaned, as if waking from a deep and ancient slumber, stretching their wooden limbs that had long been un-stretched.

Ted did not feel safe here if a tornado did happen to strike.

He sat quietly, listening to the song of nature's lament. A crescendo was on the rise.

"Ted…" It was Julia's voice that broke him from his trance. "I have it."

TWENTY-TWO

SAMANTHA HAD TWO OPTIONS—fight, or give up. They were the same two options at her disposal this entire time. She had chosen to give up and hide when she was scared, and fight when she felt her friends needed her. And they had been in need of her. But now she needed them.

Bobby was dead, Julia might be; she hadn't recently moved or made a sound that Samantha could discern, and Ted was helpless with his wrists bound once again to the radiator.

Samantha was now alone.

Her friends hadn't deserted her. Worse, she caused their absence. Everything that had happened downstairs in the living room of the old farmhouse, Samantha was to blame for it. She wouldn't—or couldn't—place the blame on anyone else. She was the one who called the police. She brought the gun that killed Bobby into the house. She brought the man here who alerted Michael of her presence. She might as well have kicked Julia in the back herself.

Samantha knew the role she'd played in all that had happened.

Michael strode forward and grabbed a fist of her limp and filthy hair, shoving her backwards so she fell onto the bed. Seeing his approach had stopped the blood in her veins. The panic that swept through her felt charged, numbing her limbs, all the way down to the ends of her fingers and the tips of her toes.

She felt the familiar pounding in her chest return when her body hit the soft sheets of the bed. The bed Michael and his wife once shared together as Mr. and Mrs. Hansen.

Michael had turned his back to grab something from the top of a dresser. Now was the time to run if she was going to, but Samantha had no control over herself. The anxiety attack had settled in and wasn't going anywhere.

Turning back to face her, Michael held in his hand a large hunting knife.

Samantha didn't know what he was going to do with it. Nothing good ever happened with knives. They had only one function, and that was to cut.

Slowly, ever so slowly, Michael leaned over Samantha and slid the tip of the knife into her ear. "The louder you scream," Michael said as he pushed the blade in a little further, just far enough to draw blood, "the deeper this goes."

The cut in her ear stung like mad. It took everything Samantha had not to cry out. She clenched her jaw tight to keep it from quivering. Her breaths came in heavy gulps without a pause in between.

In that moment, with Michael standing before her, six-inch blade in hand, no place to run and no way to fight, Samantha knew she was going to die.

She expected to see something, the life-flashing-before-her-eyes kind of thing she had always heard about on TV. All the good times she had shared with her family as a child growing up in the Pittsburgh suburbs. Her older sister and the countless memories they created together, too many to remember. Some bad times to remind her how special the good times were. Her friends at school, her neighbors, relatives. Ted. Alice. Julia and Bobby.

But she saw none of that.

She only saw Michael.

Samantha let her eyes close. If this was the end, she would see no more. Better to let those memories come, the good times and the bad, let them fade as her big sister welcomed her with open arms for them to embrace once again.

And then the panic was gone.

It was as if a weight had been lifted off her chest. She felt weightless, floating in the blackness of nothing. The world was without sight or sound. She looked every which way, looking to find her sister, to hug her and never let go.

Samantha tried calling out for Alice, but her voice would not carry. She was in a vacuum. But there was a sound, far off in the distance, around one too many corners to be understood.

She ran.

The sound grew louder. A rushing of water. A river spilling over its banks, its current screaming by. Samantha yelled and shouted, but nobody would hear. She looked and ran and tried to follow the river, but everything was moving too fast.

Rushing water spilled over to where Samantha stood. She backpedaled before the water could touch her, reeling away from the surging rapids.

She was gripped with an irresistible urge to turn around and run back the way she came. There was something in the water. She couldn't understand what it was, but she felt a fear like nothing she had ever felt before.

Her eyes shot open.

There Michael still stood, bringing the knife down on her in an overhead arc.

"Samantha!"

She was jolted back to reality at the sound of her name, and the voice that called it.

Ted rushed into the room like lightning, grabbing for the knife. Michael spun around to face his attacker and Samantha scrambled backward, falling off the bed on the opposite side to where the scuffle ensued.

Hands fumbled, fingers slipping against the blade, blood gleaming black in the pale light. Ted raised a knee to Michael's stomach, impacting hard. With a sudden exhale, the hunting knife fell from Michael's fingers and landed somewhere in the dark.

"Samantha, get out of here!" Ted shoved with all his might to clear Michael from the only doorway out of the bedroom, trying to create a gap for Samantha to run through.

Then a hand shot out, wrapping its thick and bleeding fingers around Ted's face, pushing his head back, gaining leverage.

With one quick and sudden jerk, Samantha heard the thunk of Ted's skull cracking against the wooden frame outlining the bedroom doorway. His arms fell limp and his legs dropped out from under him, and he slunk down to the floor at Michael's feet.

Samantha reacted without thinking.

She turned away from Michael, took three quick steps toward the window and jumped.

TWENTY-THREE

GLASS EXPLODED TOWARD SAMANTHA'S EYES. She raised her arms to shield her face as fierce winds ripped through her hair.

The fall lasted a mere second. There was a deck built on to the back of the house which saved her about five feet, though the unforgiving planks of wood had considerably less give than if she had landed on the soft and spongy grass that had been saturated by the storm all night long.

Samantha came down feet first, with one ankle unable to find a proper angle to meet the deck. It bent sideways, taking ligaments and tendons with it, stretching in a way a foot was never meant to stretch. She felt bone slam perpendicularly into the wood with jackhammer force.

She cried out in agony, her hands going to her ankle immediately upon landing. Samantha had never broken a bone before, so she wasn't sure if that's what had just happened, but the pain was excruciating. It could be from tearing something in her foot rather than a fracture, but Samantha naturally feared the worse.

She was scared out of her mind. Scared to the point that her thoughts were sober. There was no more assuming this or hoping for that; there was only this moment.

Her arms, she noticed, felt miraculously unharmed. There didn't appear to be any cuts or lacerations on her from the window at all. But the pain in her foot was severe, and the fall had done something to her ribs, exacerbating the damage caused when she'd slipped in the mud and fallen against that rock earlier in the day.

There was no thunder. Only the sound of the wind whipping through the trees and the rainfall pattering against the deck. Samantha pulled her hair from her face, but the storm blew it back. She had to hold it up with her hand so she could see what had happened to her foot.

By the looks of it in the dark, it seemed as if everything was still in place. She tried to move it up and down, but it felt like someone driving a hot needle into the center of her ankle.

Samantha had seen Alice break her arm when they were young. In an attempt to walk up a sliding board from the bottom, Alice had lost her balance just before reaching the top, and she fell over the side before she could grab hold of something to steady herself. Alice rarely ever cried, but she cried that day.

If I'm not crying, Samantha told herself, *then it's not broken.*

She had to move. Michael was coming for her. But where to go? The steps of the deck seemed an unconquerable challenge, and the uneven terrain beyond was out of the question, particularly in the storm.

Samantha knew her options were limited. She could try to run, but she didn't even know if she could walk. She would have to go back into the house, find the best weapon she could find, and use it.

Samantha pulled herself up to one foot, testing only

the ball of her other foot gingerly.

That wasn't going to work.

She hopped on one leg toward the back door, hoping she didn't slip in the rain and fall once more. At the door, she gave herself a second of rest, then pulled the old farmhouse door open and hopped inside.

Samantha stood in the kitchen, and standing on the opposite side of the room in the threshold of the living room was Michael. Ted lay crumpled at his feet, presumably thrown down the stairs rather than carried. He remained unconscious.

They each stood their ground without moving, Samantha and Michael, waiting for the other to act first. It reminded Samantha of the old cowboy movies her father would watch late at night when kids were supposed to be in bed. She would sneak downstairs and hide beside the big rocking chair, wondering why the two opponents would wait so long before fighting.

Now she knew.

Samantha leaned back, resting the heels of her hands on the countertop that ran around three of the four kitchen walls, edging her way toward the knife block next to the sink.

To Michael's right were the kitchen table and the doorway to the basement, still hanging open. He gave a look through that open door, debating. The state trooper's gun must be down there, Samantha realized. If he went for it, she would not have much time to run, even if Michael took his sweet time looking for it. His eyes went back to Samantha.

She maintained eye contact the whole way over to where the knife block was waiting for her, just like the cowboys in the western films. If you look away, you lose. She groped behind her, feeling for the largest handle, hoping it belonged to the largest blade.

Samantha found it curious that Michael did not hold in his hand the hunting knife that he had been wielding in the bedroom. He stood unarmed, only his coarse farmer's hands for weapons.

That made her feel a little better, but not much. He was still a formidable man who had shown himself capable of handling more physically opposing figures like Bobby and Ted, even the state trooper and the first man killed. Samantha understood that she was the omega, not the alpha. Michael would not think himself so low as to require a gun or a knife to take care of her. That would be too easy.

A crack of thunder made her jump. Michael stood as still as a statue, letting the ensuing flash of lightning wash over him, allowing Samantha a glimpse of that wry and twisted smile he wore, the gleaming in his dark and hollow eyes. The eyes of the insane.

Samantha suddenly felt weak for letting herself flinch. She had to look strong. She couldn't look weak. She couldn't *feel* weak. Michael would only feed on that. He could sense it on her like a dog, some strange aura about her that she couldn't wash away, not even after a lifetime of trying.

She felt she had to do something, show him she wasn't afraid of him. So she did the only thing she could think of—slipped the sandals off her feet, being careful with the one on her twisted ankle, which felt tighter due to some considerable swelling, holding her stare on Michael the entire time. Samantha tossed the sandals aside, out of the way.

Michael tracked their flight into the corner and gave a chuckle. "Those aren't even yours." His words boomed with a strange gravity, bestowed by a house with no other voices to join in the chorus. Life seemed absent outside of this little kitchen.

Samantha didn't say a word in reply. Her voice would only sound small, like a frightened mouse. She had to stay strong.

It grew oddly quiet. The winds had calmed, the falling rain lessened, and now all Samantha could hear was the beating of her own heart, the hoarse breaths she drew and exhaled, and the creaking of the floor beneath Michael's boots as he advanced.

Samantha whipped the knife around, holding it in front of her like a shield. Michael took another step closer. Samantha slashed the air between them. "Stop!" she yelled. "Don't come any closer!"

Michael paused, leveling a glare of menace at her. She expected another remark, a quip to demonstrate his confidence, but as the storm had grown quiet, so had Michael.

Then he grabbed a chair from beside the kitchen table with one arm and flung it toward Samantha. The chair was big and the room was small. She had nowhere to go. She raised her arms up to protect her head and the impact knocked the knife from her hand. She couldn't see where it went, but heard a clatter of metal against metal in the sink beside her.

Samantha felt herself falling with nothing to grab hold of. She landed flat on her back and all the air in her lungs rushed out of her at once.

Michael stepped forward again, heavy boots thumping

against the cold tile floor. Samantha felt a panic rising. She had to breathe. Concentrate and breathe. She scrambled to the counter and pulled herself up, ignoring the feeling of daggers in her side.

She didn't anticipate Michael going to the sink or hearing the scrape of the sharp blade against the stainless steel as he took it in his hand. Before he could turn around, Samantha leaped off of her one good foot and onto Michael's back, wrapping her arms around his thick neck and squeezing with every ounce of strength she had left.

She had not attempted to harm another person before in all her life, but she did not hold back.

The knife fell back into the sink and Samantha squeezed her arms tighter and tighter. She heard him cough and gag and wheeze as he struggled for air as she had just done on the floor. Michael's hands reached up, looking to grab Samantha and pull her away. She bit a flailing finger until she felt her teeth touch bone.

The room shook violently as Michael tried to shrug her off. She could feel the desperation in his every movement. Quick, jerky, not careful and calculated as he had been before. She had caught him by surprise.

Then Samantha felt herself moving backwards—fast. Too fast to be controlled. Michael drove back with all the momentum he could muster in such a confined area. Samantha felt the bones in her chest bend as she impacted the refrigerator, sandwiched between it and Michael.

She was too terrified to let go. There was an avalanche of sounds within the refrigerator as bottles broke and containers fell over, and Samantha heard the dripping of fluids coming out from below the door that had bounced open from the collision.

Samantha squeezed her arms even tighter. She could feel the tautness in the veins in Michael's neck, but she wasn't about to let go. She held on for dear life, silently praying for this to end.

Then she felt Michael's hands grab hold of her by the hair. With a sharp yank, Samantha flipped over his head. Her legs landed on the counter in front of them, but with no support for her upper body, she toppled backward and jackknifed into the tile floor head-first.

Michael leaned against the counter sucking dry, ragged breaths and coughing.

Samantha squirmed at his feet. The fall had knocked her dizzy, though not half as badly as when her head had cracked into the corner of the coffee table. She tried to find her footing to stand, but Michael decided to help her up the hard way—by body-slamming her onto the countertop.

A shockwave jolted her ribcage, stirring up every recent memory of how badly they had hurt only a few short hours ago. She tried to convince herself to roll off the counter and curl up in a ball on floor, its coolness a welcoming touch against her sweaty and sticky skin.

But Michael again had his sights set on the knife.

Samantha grabbed behind her, whatever solid object that was within reach—a cutting board, the heavy, wooden kind that her grandmother had loved so much. She turned to her side so she could swing with both hands. The ear-splitting *thwack* sounded like a gunshot against the back of Michael's skull.

He dropped to one knee with a heavy thud. Samantha knew she had to use this opportunity to her advantage. Looking ahead, she saw the sink at the end of the counter.

There was no energy left in her. She couldn't muster

the strength to stand up and walk a measly six feet. So she crawled. Down the counter she crawled, knocking over whatever was in her path, pulling herself along with two hands and one good foot.

Samantha crawled right over the stove-top—the sink nearly within reach.

She was so drawn by the knife that she had forgotten to look down at Michael. Had forgotten to protect herself. Michael instantly knew the mistake she had made, and turned on all the burners to the stove-top as Samantha lay across them.

Screams filled the air and smoke wafted from burning clothes and singed human flesh. Samantha writhed in the flames; every time she put a hand or knee or elbow down to push herself away, she found it burning and had to pull away.

Samantha finally rolled off the stove-top and dropped to the floor, rolling against the tiles to smother the flames on her tank-top and shorts. The smell was horrendous. She nearly vomited right then and there.

The familiar sound of metal scraping against metal rang from above. As Samantha looked up, Michael brought the knife down.

Her natural reaction was to throw a fist up and punch him square in the balls. No matter how big the man…

The knife sailed across the kitchen, coming to a clattering stop on the top of the table after bouncing off the far wall. Michael grunted a deep grunt that came from somewhere down near his stomach. A primal noise.

Profanity flew as Michael doubled over, both hands clutching between his legs. His face was redder than it had been when Samantha had him in a choke hold.

Samantha wasted but a second reviewing the damage she had just caused him. A voice inside her wailed for her to move, to get up and run for the knife. She pulled herself up to her feet and hobbled toward the table, using the countertops and refrigerator for support. She could hardly put any weight on her swollen ankle at all.

Nearly there, Samantha's hobble turned into a near-sprint. The prize was within grasp. She only had to cross the finish line. A little too much weight on her bad foot and she fell to one knee, with one hand grasping the tabletop.

The knife was within reach.

She felt her fingertips brushing against the handle…

And then it was gone. A shadow fell over her. A large hand, a farmer's hand, planted its meaty palm on her wrist, holding her hand in place.

Michael raised the knife into the air.

Samantha had scarcely a second to look up, but the blade had already come down, slamming into the wood of the old kitchen table in the same manner as a butcher chops meat.

A warming sensation shot up Samantha's left arm, all the way to her shoulder. A numbness crept in, starting with a tingle in her fingers and drifting its way up to her elbow. Her eyes fell to where the knife dropped and she saw only blood. She lifted her hand off the table, but two and a half fingers stayed where they were, on the opposite side of the blade.

Samantha fell into a seated position on the floor, her back resting against the refrigerator. She grabbed her blood-soaked hand with the other and cradled it against her shivering body.

Michael picked something up from the floor at his feet. Julia's engagement ring. He slipped it into his pocket.

Samantha heard his heavy boot steps leave the kitchen. Now the pain was growing, like thorns all around her hand, their roots burrowing deep into her wrist. She couldn't see through the cloud of tears in her eyes. She didn't want to see.

Samantha wept.

There was no more fight in her. It was beaten out of her. She was not her sister. The realization repeated over and over again in her mind, taunting her with the truth of it. She had failed. She was weak and that's why she failed. She was not her sister.

When Michael returned, he yanked Samantha's good hand up to where it rested against the handle of the refrigerator. She put up no fight. He slapped one end of the state trooper's handcuffs over Samantha's wrist and the other on the fridge door handle.

"Don't go anywhere. We're not finished yet." Michael strolled to where Ted lay at the bottom of the stairs.

Ted had not moved from the spot, but was now showing signs of consciousness. His arms moved as if in a thick liquid, as though he was remembering how to use them and what he needed to use them for.

Michael dragged him by his feet toward the front door, past where Julia was sprawled out face-down and unmoving. Past the corpses of Bobby and the state trooper and Michael's wife. Samantha turned her head to see the door opening, the two men exit, and the door slam shut.

TWENTY-FOUR

Ted awoke in a dream.

All around him was the sound of rainfall, spilling in sheets on the roof of the vehicle and against the side windows. He rocked back and forth as he was driven over an unpaved path. The world became clear, and he found himself staring at the driver from the wrong end of a cage.

This was not a dream, Ted realized. He was in the back of the state police cruiser, and Michael was driving.

Ted sat up, his skull pounding from the effort. His head felt enormous. "Where are you taking me?" He could see the house to his right and the old garage to his left.

"Just going for a ride," Michael said.

"A ride to where?" It looked to Ted that they were traveling to the rear of the home, away from the dirt path leading to the main road.

"Tell me, Ted. Can you swim?"

The question seemed odd, but Ted understood the context when the pond behind the back yard came into view. "Where is Samantha? What did you do with her?"

"She's fine. She's just resting."

Resting where? From what? Is she still alive? A million questions needed to be asked, but Ted knew Michael would supply no straight answers. It was all a game to him. From the moment Julia set foot on the front porch and peeked in the window, it was a game. A game Michael was indeed winning.

Michael piloted the state trooper's vehicle straight for the pond. Slow, not in a rush to lose control and get the wheels stuck in the slick and muddy grass. And the rain continued to pour. Thunder sounded above, like the gods pounding on firmament drums.

Yes, Ted thought. He could swim. He could swim very well, actually. But he could not unlock the back doors of a state trooper's cruiser from inside. He could not break the windows. He could not smash through the cage, and he could not call for anyone to rescue him.

Water terrified Samantha. Her sister's drowning had done something to her. The puddle she fell into after exiting the Jeep was the most water she'd seen since that day. He wondered if she was still alive…

The car pulled to a stop, its front wheels a foot from the bank.

Ted scrambled, hands bracing him against the seat. "Don't do it, Michael. This is a mistake! Trust me—"

Michael shifted into neutral. "Trust you? What cause would I have to do that? All you've done is lie to me, threaten me, assault me, and try to kill me. Sorry if all this has caused me to run low on trust."

"Just … just think. You have half a dozen bodies piled up in your living room—one of which is a cop. A state trooper."

"I know."

"This can't all just disappear."

Michael opened the driver's door a crack. "Perhaps

171

not." He stepped out, leaving the door open and peeking his head inside. "But you can."

"No, wait—Michael!" Ted's pleas went unheard.

"I'll give Samantha your regards," Michael said and, with one hand guiding the wheel, rolled the vehicle into the water.

The car plunged into the pond, bobbing there like a toy as the murky water rushed in through the open driver's side door.

Ted yanked at the cage but it would not give. He pulled his feet onto the seat, away from the water, but the level was rising fast. He pounded both feet against the window as hard as he could, but the effort was futile.

Breaths came shorter and quicker. This was a joke, he thought, a cruel joke that fate found hilarious. The man responsible for at least four deaths was walking away free as could be while Ted sank to the bottom of that man's pond—simply for being in the wrong place at the wrong time.

How could it come to this? How could he do nothing wrong and still lead his best friends to such an outcome? It wasn't fair. Life wasn't fair. It was taking all the people he cared about, and without reason. Even Alice didn't have to go. There was no reason. But she went all the same. Bobby next. Julia was at death's door, and Samantha...

"Please don't take Samantha, too. Please don't do it."

He said the words aloud to nobody. Heard or unheard, they just had to be spoken. He knew there was no way out of this vehicle. The water was up to his chin, and soon it would be over the roof of the car. That much was unavoidable.

Ted was always looked at as the guy who had an

answer for everything. He had no answer for this.

He sucked in the deepest breath he could and with the last pocket of air bubbling up to the surface, the water swallowed the vehicle with him inside.

TWENTY-FIVE

THE BLEEDING HAD SLOWED. That was good.

Samantha held a bag of frozen vegetables she had found in the freezer against the wound where her fingers used to be. She couldn't decide if she felt numbness or a throbbing pulse aching to be mended.

Her shirt hung heavier than before. Rainfall from when she fell outside coupled with the accumulating blood in her lap drenched the fabric. It was all over her shorts, too. She didn't know what 'a lot' meant in terms of blood loss, but she knew that's how much blood she had lost. A lot.

It was in this moment when she realized the storm had started up again. Rain fell in buckets. It had rained all afternoon and all evening. How was that even possible? There was no clock to be seen, so she had no clue what time it was. It could be 6:00pm or midnight. The thunder and lightning had moved on, it seemed. Taking their place was a wind more ferocious than before.

Samantha lifted her head at the sound of what she could only assume was the side of the house preparing to collapse. She had never heard old wood move in such a way. But nothing had fallen. Nothing had caved in on her.

She wanted to feel thankful for that, but there was little to be thankful for in her current state—shackled to a murderer's refrigerator with ribs likely broken, an ankle that continued to swell, a migraine that made the world unsteady, second-degree burns on her elbows and knees, and two and a half of her fingers sitting on the kitchen table.

What was there to be thankful for?

Her friends were dead. Her best friend was just dragged outside for reasons Samantha did not know, but a sense that she would never see him again persisted. Her parents had no idea what was happening. She had called them three times every day to let them know where she was and how the trip was going. They were probably worried out of their minds by now, but they couldn't do anything about it.

The thought brought a rush of emotions to the surface, and tears were soon streaming down Samantha's face. They had already lost one daughter; they couldn't stand to lose another. She knew they would be devastated. And it was her fault. All her own fault.

All because she was weak.

Samantha was too weak to save Alice, too weak to save Ted, too weak to save Julia or Bobby, too weak to save Mrs. Hansen, and too weak to save the state trooper.

If anything, she caused them more harm by trying to help than if she'd simply cowered in a corner afraid.

Maybe this was her punishment for trying to be someone she wasn't. She was supposed to be the quiet, passive girl who didn't take chances, the meek and timid one guided by fear. That was her job, and when she chose not to do it, she screwed everything up for everyone else.

Is that life? Is this how we know when we've done some-thing wrong? Samantha didn't know. At twenty-two years old, she had never assumed she knew much about life. Her experiences were quite limited—a fact she became aware of while attending her big sister's funeral. There was a way things moved in life, it seemed, but the path was unclear.

As Samantha grew older, less and less made sense. For how magnificent and full of wonder the world seems to children, it all fits together and feels whole, feels like there's a reason for everything. But what was the reason for this? Why was it ending this way? Samantha questioned whether or not she had done anything wrong. It didn't feel that way. Certainly nothing that could possibly warrant this. If she had done nothing wrong, then what was the reason? Did she upset the balance of order when she tried to push her fears aside and act instead of flee?

Samantha had herself convinced that she had this level of control over the world when she heard the sound of a vehicle driving around to the back of the house.

She lifted her head, but there were no windows affording a view of what was happening. Slowly, she stood, holding the frozen vegetables to her stomach with her injured hand, the handcuffs sliding up the length of the fridge door handle as she rose.

The state trooper's vehicle pulled into view, headlights throwing a wash of light through the darkness toward the large pond nestled just beyond the back yard.

Samantha strained to see who occupied the vehicle. There were two heads she saw for certain. Michael and Ted.

Michael's motive became clear to Samantha—he was going to dispose of the car and Ted in one fell swoop. Then he would come inside and do the same with Bobby and Julia. Throw them into the pond or bury them in the basement. Next, he would get rid of the body of the state trooper, saving his wife for last, and forcing Samantha to watch through it all, torturing her.

Samantha gave a feeble tug at the handcuffs. There was no way to get out of them unless she had a key. But there was nothing in reach. She was trapped.

There was no more fight in her. She slid down to the floor and sat again. If there was one thing she could be thankful for, she thought, it was the fact that she didn't have to watch Ted suffer any longer.

She felt a strange lump in her back pocket. She leaned to the side, thinking she had sat on something, a piece of debris from the kitchen brawl moments ago, perhaps. But there was nothing on the floor beneath her besides a puddle of assorted fluids and bits of glass.

Then she remembered.

It was the screwdriver she had tucked away in her back pocket the whole time. She fished it out with two fingers from her injured hand. Flat head. She might be able to pick the lock on the cuffs.

Samantha fumbled with the object, using her chin, her teeth, whatever she could to help stabilize it enough to fit it in the lock like a thread through the eye of a needle.

But the tip of the screwdriver was too big. It would not fit into the lock.

It seemed as if the room had deflated, drawing out all energy and hope. As Samantha sat there, screwdriver gripped between two fingers, she felt that something wasn't right. She was going to get free. There had to be a way. And, all of a sudden, giving up was no longer an option. It wasn't a conscious decision; she just knew there was a way.

There *had* to be a way.

Outside, the state trooper's vehicle crashed into the pond.

Samantha stood. Michael was walking back to the house, and Ted was sinking along with the car.

She jerked at the handcuffs, but they wouldn't budge. The chain was too strong to force apart with the screwdriver, and, with a hobbled hand, Samantha was too weak.

Then she had a thought. It was an old style refrigerator, with the freezer on the bottom. Samantha knelt and pulled the fridge door open, looking under the door at the screws that held the handle in place.

TWENTY-SIX

SHE KNEW THAT THE ONLY way to the back yard without being seen was through the basement and out the door she had entered earlier that day.

There was no light on in the basement, but Samantha found her way in the dark, remembering how the floor was laid out. She followed the sound of rainfall to the old, weather-beaten door and yanked it open.

Above, Samantha heard heavy footfalls as Michael entered the house from the back door.

Time was limited. By now, he knew she was gone, and the first place he would look was out the little window behind the sink.

The rain fell in torrents and the wind screamed, beating against Samantha's face as she ran as fast as her broken body would carry her, making a beeline for the pond.

She wanted to look back to see where Michael was, how close on her heels he was bound to be. But she didn't. She kept her eyes straight ahead, looking at the pond and only the pond.

There were a thousand other things Samantha wanted to do, and diving into the water was at the bottom of that list. If she thought about it, she knew she would falter. She would hesitate, and Ted would drown. She just had to take a deep breath and dive in.

She dove into the pond.

It took precious seconds for her eyes to adjust, but below the murky haze was the glow of taillights. She swam hard, harder than she knew she could. It was too dark to see Ted inside. Samantha fumbled blindly for the door handle.

When she found it, she grabbed hold and pulled with all her strength.

She didn't know what to expect. Her ribs were in agony from holding her breath. She pushed herself into the back of the vehicle, but the next thing she knew, she was moving toward the surface. She had to breathe, but Ted was still in there...

They broke the surface together, gasping for air, wind whipping at their faces.

"Come on!" Ted coughed up water and pulled Samantha onto land and they ran for the cellar door.

The wind was loud. Too loud. Samantha knew something was wrong, but Ted had her by the hand, dragging her toward shelter. He must know, too.

"Get inside, quick!" Ted kicked the door open and shoved Samantha inside.

"Not so fast, Ted." Michael had to scream over the sound. Ted saw the shotgun in Michael's hands and froze where he stood.

Samantha looked out to see why Ted wasn't coming inside. Before she saw the man with the shotgun, she saw the tornado.

Dirt and debris swirled in a colossal whirlwind as nature carved a path through whatever was in its way.

Structures blasted into splinters and trees snapped like dry twigs. And it was coming straight for Michael's farmhouse.

"This is insane!" Ted screamed. "You're going to get us all killed!"

"Might be," Michael shouted. "But it has to end somehow."

Samantha turned, eyes hurriedly scanning for something, anything that could help…

And then she found it.

She raced to the handgun that had fallen down the stairs, grabbed it in her hand and limped back to the door. Every step carried the thought that the next sound she would hear would be the deafening blast of the shotgun.

The farmhouse above her head groaned as century-old dust fell on her head from between boards that had never before moved. Shelves wobbled, half their items spilling onto the concrete floor.

Samantha heard shouted voices as she neared the doorway…

"We have to go inside!"

"Stay right where you are. And where's the other one? Your girl…"

Samantha leaned out from behind the doorway. "Right here." She aimed the gun at Michael and squeezed the trigger.

The shotgun fell as the bullet slammed into Michael's chest, and his body tumbled backwards down the porch steps.

The gun fell from Samantha's shaking fingers. She may have just killed a man.

Ted grabbed her by the shoulders and pulled her inside. The tornado was just beyond the pond.

The last thing Samantha saw was Michael's hand reach up, pawing for the stairs, trying in desperation to pull himself up. Then there was again darkness as Ted shoved the door closed.

They ducked into the concrete room under the porch—the room where the adulterous man was buried. Samantha felt her ears pop. The pressure was like nothing she had ever felt before.

Huddled in the corner, she closed her eyes and covered her ears as the world was ripped apart piece by piece just above her head. The floor would collapse, and they would be dead, too, she was certain. Hands pressed against her ears as hard as she could did nothing to block the cacophony of rending walls, floors torn up, and the wind…

It had happened faster than she thought possible.

TWENTY-SEVEN

WHEN SAMANTHA OPENED HER EYES, she felt like she was waking up from a long nap. Her vision came into focus and the room was the same as it was moments ago. Or hours ago? She had no semblance of time.

It was then she realized that her arms were around Ted and his around her. Their eyes met, but no words were exchanged. They watched and waited, scanning the room, listening. For what, Samantha couldn't say. Everything was quiet.

Ted's eyes fell to her injured hand. It was still moist with fresh blood. "Here," he said, and pulled his shirt off. He wrapped Samantha's hand, taking care to put pressure on the wounds while causing as little pain as he could.

They got to their feet and took cautious steps out of the room. The basement was disheveled, as if it had been picked up, held upside-down, and shaken. And the stairs leading to the first floor still stood.

Samantha reached the top of the steps and entered a different place than before. The kitchen was gone, leaving little trace that it had ever been there. Turning, she saw that the second floor had collapsed on the living room. Only a pile of splintered wood and random broken objects remained.

Julia was under that pile, Samantha knew. There was no way she had survived.

Only one wall still stood on the first floor, supporting the fraction of the upstairs that had not been taken away. Samantha craned her head back and looked up into the open night sky.

The rainfall had passed and a silence had fallen. She heard no sound at all. Nothing falling, nothing dripping, nothing rustling in the property of the farm. Not even the sound of a bird.

Ted navigated the destruction, making for where the front porch once stood. In its place was his Jeep, half-buried in the front bedroom that was once nine feet higher.

Samantha followed Ted's lead, careful where she placed her bare feet. Broken wood covered the floor. She looked, but found no sign of the floor itself. The house that once stood right there had been disintegrated.

The only door Ted found access to on the Jeep was the rear hatch, jutting out of the rubble at a forty-five degree angle. He gave a tug. Locked.

Something ahead caught his eye, and he stepped off the home's foundation and into the front yard.

Samantha hobbled through the disaster, climbing over little hills built from parts of the walls and furniture. She stepped off the front porch and onto solid ground. Every direction she looked, there was catastrophe. From little bits of the home to large sections of what was once the garage, to unidentifiable objects, to a boat that had randomly placed itself in the front yard… It would take months to clear all this.

She passed a tree stripped of its bark. Half of its limbs were shorn clean off of the trunk and nowhere to be found.

There were voices on the air, distant impressions, men and women calling out names of loved ones who could not be found. One at first, then two, then more.

Ted found Michael's disfigured corpse deposited in a hedgerow, half-buried in thorns. He searched the pockets and pulled out an object he did not expect to find—Julia's ring. He slid it in his own pocket and searched Michael again before finding what he was looking for.

He took the keys to his Jeep and walked over to where Samantha stood in the center of the front yard, crippled hand cradled against her body, head cast down, not wanting to see any more ruin.

When Ted approached, he wrapped his arms around her and held her head close to his chest. "You saved my life," he said with tears behind his voice.

Samantha knew of no words to describe what she was feeling in that moment. But as they walked in the direction of police and ambulance sirens calling from the highway, she knew one thing…

She wasn't afraid anymore.

Made in the USA
Monee, IL
13 April 2020